TESSA

TESSA

BARBARA STEINER

MORROW JUNIOR BOOKS / NEW YORK

Inquiries should be addressed to
William Morrow and Company, Inc.
105 Madison Avenue
New York, NY 10016.

Printed in the United States of America.
1 2 3 4 5 6 7 8 9 10
Library of Congress Cataloging-in-Publication Data
Steiner, Barbara A.
Tessa.

Summary: Turning fourteen in 1946 brings several
unwanted changes for Tessa as her long-standing
friendship with a black boy is threatened and her
parents' separation forces her to choose between
living with her mother in the city or staying with
her father in the Arkansas woods and hunting for
Indian relics.
[1. Parent and child—Fiction. 2. Divorce—Fiction.
3. Arkansas—Fiction] I. Title.
PZ7.S825Te 1988   [Fic]   87-31524
ISBN 0-688-07232-1

In memory of my daddy: Hershel Thomas Daniel

If you forget where you come from,
it's easy to forget where you want to go.

Anonymous

CHAPTER
ONE

Spring was Tessa Mae's favorite time of year. Someone had raised every window in the classroom and the sounds and smells of May wafted in, making her miserable. It seemed such a waste of time to be inside with spring going on in the woods.

She felt trapped behind a desk that seemed too small for her. Her saddle shoes pinched—the same shoes she'd been so pleased to get in January. She put one foot in the aisle, noticing that the tip of the shoe was gray instead of white and that there was a deep scratch along the side. She could feel her big toe pushing against the leather, begging to be freed. She felt every bit as imprisoned as that toe.

As Tessa Mae leaned over to loosen the shoe laces, her faded calico dress stretched across her back and chest and her strawberry blond hair tumbled down around her face.

On such a fine day her daddy was most likely down on the river bottoms. She wished she was with him. She wished she had the nerve to take her freedom the way he always had. No one in the classroom would miss her if she left. Miss Criswell would know she was gone, but nice as she was to Tessa Mae, she didn't think the young teacher would *miss* her. For a moment she felt sorry for Miss Criswell, struggling to explain Thoreau to people like Erline Crider and Chester Wilcox.

Tessa Mae loved the parts of *Walden* they'd read. What Mr. Thoreau had written spoke to her, much more than Mr. Frank Slaughter, whose books gave her a funny feeling in the pit of her stomach, and Mr. Paul Wellman, who left her wanting to go back in history and have an adventure of her own. Of course, those books were made up. Mr. Henry David Thoreau had really done the things he wrote about. She envied his running off to live in the woods away from town, building his own house on that pond, sitting there watching the animals and birds.

Miss Criswell had asked each student to write a paragraph about living alone in the woods. Tessa Mae's paper was blank except for the date: May 10, 1946, and her name: Tessa Mae Ferris.

"All right, class." Miss Criswell was still trying to get some responses to her questions. "What do you think Thoreau meant when he said, 'Time is but the stream I go a-fishing in'? "

Miss Criswell ignored the raised hands. "Tessa Mae, what do you think he meant?"

Tessa Mae met the teacher's gaze defiantly, choosing not to talk although she knew the answer:

Time goes on forever, she thought, and we pull out little pieces to use up any way we please. Even her friend Jec would know that. Jec was only twelve to her fourteen, but he was every bit as good a reader as she and better at math. He had helped her with fractions this year.

"She's forgot you're deaf and dumb," whispered Chester Wilcox, who sat behind her. Tessa Mae ignored him too. Chester had grown so fast this spring that his wrists and hands dangled naked from his shirt sleeves and his jeans were too short. He hung around Tessa Mae all the time, grinning and smelling sweaty.

Finally Miss Criswell gave up on her, and she called on Ralph Willey who was waving his hand like a flag in the breeze.

"You forget what time it is when you're fishing." Ralph grinned, pleased with his answer. "You don't even know there's such a thing as time."

"That's true, Ralph. I can see you're a patient fisherman. Erline, do you have another idea?"

Erline Crider sat two seats in front of Tessa Mae—on the front row. She'd talk the whole period if Miss Criswell would let her.

"No, I just wanted to read my paragraph." Erline adjusted the ribbon in her hair, stood, and cleared her throat. "I can't think of anything worse than living off in the woods by yourself. I'd really hate it. You wouldn't get to see any picture shows, and what good would a new dress be? No one would see it. You probably wouldn't even get to go to church if you had to walk two miles. I think Mr. Henry David Thoreau was a little crazy, or maybe he never got along with anyone anyway. So he figured he'd go off alone."

Chester giggled and poked Tessa Mae as Erline turned, gave the class a smug look, then sat down. "I'll bet Erline would walk two miles just to show off a new dress, don't you?" he whispered.

Tessa Mae figured Chester was right about Erline, but she didn't let on that she'd heard him. She bent and laced her shoes, relieved class was almost over.

"Well, Erline, that's interesting," said Miss Criswell. "And you're entitled to your opinion. Not everyone would enjoy living in the woods alone. We have a few minutes left, class. I'll read all your papers if you'll put them on my desk as you leave, but I'd like to hear what you think Thoreau means when he says: 'My instinct tells me that my head is an organ for burrowing, as some creatures use their snout and fore paws, and with it I would mine and burrow my way through these hills.' "

No one volunteered until Erline spoke up. "Just what I already said. The man was strange."

The class was glad to laugh. It was nearly lunch time, and they were all hot and hungry.

Miss Criswell let the giggles die out naturally. "Chester?" she said finally.

"The only thing I know of that roots around in the dirt is a pig, Miss Criswell. I can't see no good in it."

Tessa Mae was disgusted with the whole discussion. "Oh, fer goodness sakes," she blurted out. "Mr. Thoreau meant you kin learn a lot about life by wanderin' in the woods, pokin' your nose into everythin' that goes on. You kin read everything that happens in the woods jist like you kin read a book. I kin tell when a doe is carryin' a fawn by her tracks bein' deeper in the mud, and that we was going to have a bad winter because the squirrels was busier than usual and the raccoon coats was heavy. I kin tell who used to live down by the river and what kind of people they was by the relics I kin dig up."

In her exasperation Tessa Mae had forgotten her vow never to talk like a country hick. Her face got hot, and she stared at her fingernails, dirty and ragged from digging in the dirt, looking for Indian relics the day before. She was a country hick all right, and everybody knew it.

When she first met Miss Criswell, she knew that people away from Lamar, even those who came from the bigger cities in Arkansas, didn't talk like her and her daddy and his kinfolk. And she resolved to learn to speak like the young teacher. Now she realized that not only had she forgotten to talk correctly, she'd practically given a lecture in talking wrong.

"I guess Mr. Thoreau isn't the only strange person who ever lived." Erline pounced on Tessa Mae's embarrassed silence, and her friends responded with giggles and titters as the bell rang at last.

"That's enough, class. You're dismissed. Be sure you hand in your papers." Miss Criswell watched as the eighth grade English class filed past her.

"Thank you for sharing, Tessa Mae," she called out. Tessa Mae didn't reply. She hurried out the door to her locker. Her throat ached and her chest felt as if it was full of sweet gum burrs.

"Hey, Tessa Mae." There was Erline Crider, surrounded by three other eighth grade girls. "Maybe you'd be *jist* the one to try Mr. Thoreau's experiment." Erline mocked her and was rewarded by her gang with peals of laughter. "Livin' out there in the woods alone, rootin' around with your nose into everythin'."

"Yeah, maybe you kin go pokin' around, lookin' for pregnant deer." Sue Anne Sparks giggled at saying the word *pregnant* and the others followed her lead.

Tessa Mae took the locker key from the string around her neck, snapped the lock free and jerked open the locker door. She pulled out her lunch and the sack with her gym clothes in it; then she threw in all her books and slammed the door shut.

Trying not to show how upset she was, she headed for the front door of Lamar Junior High. She paused on the steps long enough to shake off any last-minute hesitations about what she was about to do, then hurried down Maple Street towards home.

When she passed the laundry where her mother worked, washing other people's dirty clothes, she practically broke into a run. The last thing she needed was to have her mother see her, or Dixie Lee Tooley or another of her mother's friends to see her and tattle.

By the time she reached the end of town, Tessa Mae was practically dancing. If she'd have known she'd feel this good about playing hookey, she'd have done it before. But she felt guilty at not stopping to see her Uncle Elbert and Aunt Maudie. Uncle Elbert was her daddy's older brother who'd been crippled by polio for as long as Tessa Mae could remember. Aunt Maudie had to stay home all the time to take care of him. They didn't get many visitors, and Tessa Mae stopped as often as she could.

Telling herself she could spare a few minutes from her precious afternoon, she turned off Maple and skipped down an alley overlooking a cornfield to the little white house that was her second home.

"Howdy, Aunt Maudie." Tessa Mae never bothered to knock on the back door. She entered to find that Aunt Maudie had wheeled Uncle Elbert up to the kitchen table for lunch.

"Howdy, Tessa Mae. Ain't it early for you to be out of school?" Uncle Elbert reached for a slice of white bread with his twisted hand.

"There's a teachers' meetin' today. Ain't that lucky?"

Tessa Mae lied easily. She knew *ain't* wasn't good English anymore than *kin* and *jist*, but she figured there was one language for family. If she talked like Miss Criswell here, they might feel that Tessa Mae thought she was better than they were.

Aunt Maudie got up from the table. "You want some lunch? There's plenty." She always saw to it that there was more than enough good food at her house in case company dropped in. That was the way of most hill people.

"I'll have me a glass of that iced tea if you don't mind, Aunt Maudie, but I'll eat my sack lunch instead of yer food."

"Well, I've got some fresh apple cake if you don't have enough in that little old brown bag." Aunt Maudie smiled, knowing Tessa Mae's mother didn't have much time to bake.

It wasn't until she started eating that Tessa Mae realized she was starving. The ache in her throat disappeared and the tightness in her chest dropped away as if they had never been there. She leaned back in the chair and smiled.

"Uncle Elbert, tell me again about how my daddy hid his school books on his way to school."

Uncle Elbert grinned and grasped his cup of coffee with both hands because one didn't have enough strength; he sipped it and then set it back down. "Well, your daddy was not any too fond of the schoolroom. Every year the teacher would issue all the new books the first day of school. Roy Glen would take them home and have them read in a week's time. So goin' and sittin' there, listenin' to us dummies stumble over what he already knew, seemed a powerful waste of time to him."

"So what did he do?" Tessa Mae coached him, laughing, even though she knew the story by heart.

"Well, most days—the good weather ones—he'd hide those old books on our way to school. Then he'd spend the day diggin' in the river bottoms, huntin' Indian relics. We never dreamed he'd turn that into his job. He's still down there diggin'. It's like he never grew up."

"What if you had a test?" asked Tessa Mae, pretending this was the first time she'd ever heard of her daddy playing hookey.

"If we was goin' to have a test, I'd tell Roy Glen. He'd come in pretty as you please and make a hundred percent every time. You see, he'd read the assignments and worked the math problems. It wasn't as if he didn't know the work." Uncle Elbert laughed. He loved to tell stories about Roy Glen as much as Tessa Mae loved to hear them.

"And what if the gypsies came to town?" Tessa Mae took a big bite of the apple cake Aunt Maudie had set in front of her. Bite-sized chunks of pecan crunched between her teeth, the apples were moist and chewy, and cinnamon and cloves danced on her tongue. She smiled her appreciation to Aunt Maudie as Uncle Elbert continued.

"Well, Roy Glen was powerful good friends with the gypsy people. He'd cut school and go find their camp. Later he'd tell me all their stories about their travels and about their food and the music till I wished I had the nerve to run off with him."

"Why didn't you?" Tessa Mae asked.

"I guess I was afraid. And besides I wasn't as smart as Roy Glen. I had to study my books every day, and even then I got mostly *C*'s on my tests. It don't seem fair, does it?"

Tessa Mae chased the last crumb of cake across her flowered plate. Aunt Maudie loved pretty dishes and often spent the money her children sent her for extra sets, since Uncle Elbert's pension money didn't buy them many luxuries. "I guess some people can learn as much rootin' around in the woods and in gypsy camps as they would keepin' their noses in school books."

Despite what she'd said, Tessa Mae believed in books. She longed for summer so she could sit under the grape arbor and read what she pleased; historical novels were her favorites. She'd determined to read all the books in the classroom library until she found herself going back to favorites in *A* or *B* before she could get to *C* or *D*. She knew she'd never get past that whole row of Mr. Charles Dickens anyway. Often she skipped to the end of the alphabet to *S* and *W* for Mr. Irving Stone and Mr. Paul Wellman, reading whatever tempted her at the time until she had read all the ones she thought she'd enjoy.

The books set her dreaming about the adventures she'd have if she were a man. She'd ride off on a horse to explore the backwoods of Arkansas. Or go even farther to the Amazon River, or even to India to see tigers as much at home there as a mountain lion would be in the Ozarks. These were things she could talk to her daddy about—going off by herself and exploring. She thought that was why he liked looking for Indian relics. It was the closest he could come to discovering new lands.

Her mama said they were both foolish dreamers and maybe she was right, but it sure beat working in the laundry, Tessa Mae thought, or keeping track of a passel of kids. She hated to think that's what she'd end up doing.

"Thanks for the cake, Aunt Maudie. And the iced tea. I have to go." Tessa Mae jumped up from the table. "There's lots to do on a half day off from school." She waved to the older couple and hurried out the screened door, hesitating only long enough to catch it with her bottom so it wouldn't slam. Then she set off towards home, taking a short cut through the woods.

As soon as she was away from the road, Tessa Mae skinned off her tight dress. Then she pulled on her blue gym bloomers and her white blouse. She tied the bottom of the blouse into a knot so her middle was bare. Off came the saddle shoes and socks. Stuffing the shoes and dress into the paper bag, wrinkled and soft like old leather from two weeks at school, she pushed the bag under a wild hydrangea bush. The thought that maybe her daddy had put his school books under the same bush made her laugh out loud.

Jeeah, a blue jay slurred harshly, then sang out, *Helio, helio, helio*.

"Hush up," she called back, imagining that the jay was scolding her for playing hookey. "What do you know about school rooms and dumb people thinking yer crazy?"

If she *was* strange like Mr. Henry David Thoreau, she was proud of it. She'd been stupid today, letting those kids make her angry enough to talk in class instead of keeping her mouth shut as was her usual way.

"That old Thoreau would have loved my woods," she called to a gray squirrel, "wouldn't he? He'd have packed up and moved right in." Stopping to examine a red cedar tree, she pulled off an ice-blue berry and inhaled its pungent smell, then skirted a scrubby fringe of oak that threatened to take over the trail.

The dirt on the worn path felt soft and powdery to her bare feet, tender because she had worn shoes all winter. She guessed she'd have to put her shoes back on and go back to that school on Monday, but she resolved not to think about it any more today.

The sunny places in the woods were butter-yellow with coriopsis, and the smell of the wax myrtle teased her nose. Fragrant verbena waved its deep rose blossoms. A cardinal whistled and flashed by like a wind-blown scarlet ribbon. *What cheer, what cheer, what cheer, cheer, cheer.*

"What cheer yerself, old red bird?" she questioned back, dropping down on the mossy bank of the river. Yessir, she could nose around down here forever.

Tessa Mae turned on her belly, watching the water flow by, fast and muddy because of the spring rains. There was no rushing here. No bells ringing to say do this, do that. There was no one to force her to reveal her thoughts out loud. As she studied the river, burbling and chuckling past her in a constant stream, she appreciated how wise Thoreau had been. Here, time was constant. Here was where she belonged. She could afford to let the time flow by, because there was always more. Whatever consequences she had to accept about skipping school would be worth this sense of peace.

CHAPTER
TWO

Tessa Mae lay on the riverbank, inviting the solitude to fill every corner of her body and mind. She thought about the happiness Aunt Maudie and Uncle Elbert took for themselves in spite of their trouble. She thought about how important freedom had been to her daddy even when he was a boy, and how his life was still free and easy. Right now he was probably digging or just sitting, whiling away the time as he thought about where he'd look for relics next. She needed to find him, needed the reassurance that the way he chose to live was fine. So up she jumped, walking briskly along the river.

It was cool here, and she breathed in the damp, earthy smells. A shady stillness was punctuated only by the occasional buzz of a bee or mayfly. As she dodged the scratchy blackberry bushes she remembered the taste of blackberry pie and her mouth watered. She didn't want it to be time for blackberries, though. Summer was just taking hold. She had plans to carry out and aimless days to wander through.

About a mile down the river was a clearing where Roy Glen frequently camped. From that central location he could dig on either side of the river, since it settled into a lazy meander and was easy to cross. Tessa Mae was in luck. There he sat on a log on the riverbank, a cigarette pinched between two nicotine-stained fingers.

"Howdy, Roy Glen. Watching time go by?" Tessa Mae flopped down beside him.

"I reckon. It don't move very fast down here."

"That's what that feller Thoreau said." Tessa Mae figured her daddy was on the same time schedule as Thoreau.

"Thoreau? Is that one of yer schoolteachers?"

Tessa Mae laughed. "He's been one of yer teachers and mine, too, for a long time now." She told her daddy about Thoreau and about time being the fishing hole. "Once Mr. Thoreau said he was a neighbor to the birds. He hadn't put himself in a prison cage like some people do but 'he had caged himself up in a house and the birds flew free around him.' "

"You read those things in that school?" Roy Glen tossed his cigarette butt into the current. "School must be some better than when I was there."

"Not much. But I could bring you the readin's on that feller Thoreau if you'd care to think on it."

"I reckon my schoolin' days is over, Tessa Mae."

"I don't think a person's schoolin' days is ever over, Roy Glen. Sittin' in the classroom gets over, I hope, but not the learnin'. Have you ever heard of a tantivy of wild pigeons? Mr. Thoreau said that. It's my new word for today. Tantivy. I like the music of it, don't you?"

"I reckon it's a good word, but I'd feel foolish sayin' it to yer mama. Hey, Vinnie. Today I saw a tantivy of wild pigeons." Roy Glen grinned at Tessa Mae.

"She'd just about wet her pants laughin' at us, wouldn't she?" Tessa Mae figured her mother would laugh, all right. Then she'd more than likely start complaining about the two of them watching pigeons go by.

"I did see a tantivy of turkeys today." Roy Glen had run out of store-bought cigarettes and was rolling his own. Carefully he sifted golden brown tobacco into a thin paper, then pulled the drawstring that closed the tobacco bag with his teeth. He folded over the paper and tobacco and shaped it into a roll, then licked the edge of the paper. Holding the misshapen tube of tobacco, he ran his long finger across its length to seal it, then pinched one end shut. When he had lit the cigarette and taken a couple of drags, he finished his reporting of the day's events. "A big blue racer crossed the path right in front of me."

"I reckon spring is truly almost over. I missed a lot of it."

They sat in silence for a time, watching and listening. A chickadee whistled, *fee-bee*, the first note higher than the last, then shrilled, *chickadee-dee-dee*. Somewhere in the distance a pileated woodpecker hammered.

"I made a fool of myself again today, Roy Glen," Tessa Mae said. "Right before class was over. So I gave it up and left at noon."

"How'd you make a fool of yourself, Tessa Mae?"

Tessa Mae told him about Miss Criswell's question and Chester's dumb answer. "I got so disgusted that I made me a speech, all about how much there is to learn down here that's probably not in any book—any that I know of. Everyone in that school thinks I'm crazy, and I just keep provin' it for them."

"I reckon it don't matter none what people thinks if a person is happy with himself." Roy Glen took out his knife and began to whittle on a dead hickory limb.

"Mama sure don't agree with that, Roy Glen. What people thinks makes a powerful difference to her."

"You've got a lot of your mother inside of you, Tessa Mae, even though you and me don't always go along with some of her notions."

Tessa Mae didn't think she had any of her mother in her and she wasn't even sure she liked the idea. "How come you think I'm like Mama, Roy Glen?"

"Well, I'd sure never have spoke up like you did and set everyone straight. I'd of kept my thinkin' to myself." A little pile of hickory curls mounded up at Roy Glen's feet. The fresh wood smell blended with that of tobacco smoke.

"Usually I do, 'cause I'm findin' out that my thinkin' gets me in trouble. Thinkin' I could take the afternoon off will probably get me in a powerful lot of trouble."

"I guess I could write a note sayin' I needed your help this afternoon."

"Yeah, watchin' tantivies of turkeys." Tessa Mae laughed.

"And turtles." Roy Glen pointed to a mud turtle that was looking over the situation of the fast-moving, muddy water.

"No, turtles don't rush. Tantivy means rush, Roy Glen."

"Well, pardon me, Miss Know-it-all. Are you that smart-alecky at school?"

"Nope, just strange." Tessa Mae laughed.

They studied the river's passing again, and Tessa Mae savored the wholeness of the afternoon.

"I reckon I'll take me a swim before dinner," she said finally. "How about you, Roy Glen?" Tessa Mae knew that her daddy would never go swimming with her, but she felt she should ask.

"I got me some more thinkin' to do, Tessa Mae. Guess

I'll pass up the swimmin'. You have fun and watch out some big snappin' turtle doesn't get yer toe."

There weren't any big snapping turtles in the swimming hole, and Roy Glen knew it, but Tessa Mae laughed anyway. Scrambling up a dry creek bed which joined the river, she watched a broad-headed skink scurry away, then hiked back towards home. The swimming hole she favored was on the way, near Jec's house. So she decided she'd go hunt him up.

To the world, Jec was Jeconiah Claudius Brown. She figured he was the only friend she had unless you counted Roy Glen. She didn't think there was any rule about not having your daddy for a friend. But as much as Tessa Mae's mother disapproved of her hanging around down on the river bottoms with her daddy, she disapproved even more of Tessa Mae being friends with Jec. It wasn't only that Jec was a boy. He was a colored boy.

"You got to quit hangin' around down at Bertha's, Tessa Mae," her mother kept warning her. "It's not proper fer you to play with Jec now that yer growin' up. Folks in town will talk about you bein' down there so much."

Bertha Brown had cleaned, washed, and ironed for Tessa Mae's mother for as long as Tessa Mae could remember. Now that Jec was twelve, Bertha had stopped bringing Jec with her but she'd never said that Tessa Mae and her son couldn't be friends anymore.

Pushing away the thought, Tessa Mae stepped off the path into a clearing where a dozen small frame houses squatted on piles of rocks above a crawl space. This branch of the Arkansas River had been known to flood, and the houses had been built to accommodate the overflow. It hadn't happened since Tessa Mae could remember, but Roy Glen told her that in 1935 the river had risen so high it would have wiped out the houses if they had been sitting on the ground. Right now chickens rooted in the dark crawl spaces, and the cool shadows probably housed spiders and snakes. Tessa Mae and Jec had once crawled all the way under his house and out the back on a dare, and sometimes Jec hid there when Bertha was angry.

Tessa Mae could see three of Jec's sisters working in the garden behind the house, probably getting early peas for supper. Last week Bertha had said that their pole beans were coming fast too. Tessa Mae hoped she was around when Bertha cooked up the first mess of beans with bacon or salt pork.

Jec's house was the biggest in the neighborhood by two rooms, which his daddy had added on after the last three children were born. Jec counted six brothers and sisters in his family. Tessa Mae, who was an only child, couldn't imagine being one of seven, but Jec seemed to manage it. He said it meant his mother paid less attention to him.

Jec was the nearest thing to a brother that Tessa Mae had. He was twelve and she was fourteen, close enough in age to share the pleasures of swimming and fishing and poking around down in the woods on a Saturday or after school. Jec's sister, Florella, was Tessa Mae's age, but she had never felt as close to Florella as she had to Jec.

She shooed away Jec's rust-colored hen as she got closer to the house, but the hen clucked and kept scratching in the dirt with her scrawny yellow feet.

"Jec," she called out toward the window of the bedroom he shared with Rose Ann and Dee-Dee. "Come on out here. I know you're in there, hiding from any work that Florella might think up."

"Hush, Tessa Mae." Jec's face appeared at the open window. "I got me some other things to do besides pick peas or tie up beans."

"Like swimmin'? That's what I got in mind. Come on."

"Well, I was fixin' to go fishin' if you need to know."

"Take a swim first. I got to get home and start supper. You'll have plenty of time left to catch a mess of fish."

"I don't know, Tessa Mae." Jec looked worried.

"Got anything to eat, Jec?" Tessa Mae asked, ignoring Jec's expression. It seemed like weeks since lunch. Tessa Mae's head might forget about time, but her stomach had a way of reminding her.

"Come on in. I'll look," he said, then disappeared.

Tessa Mae skipped up the steps and into the cool darkness of the kitchen. Jec was already there, peeking under a bowl on the back of the stove. "Only corn bread, and I know you don't like that," he teased.

"Not much. Your mama makes the best corn bread in Arkansas."

Jec unearthed a couple of pieces of cold bacon and made them each a sandwich. Tessa Mae bit into the salty goodness, then sighed.

"I was about to fade away." She licked the crumbs from her fingers, then looked at Jec. "Ready?"

"I'm not supposed to leave the house, Tessa Mae." Jec stared at his bare feet.

"I ain't never heard of you mindin' a rule like that before." Tessa Mae sensed that Jec was lying but she didn't know why. "You get around your mama as good as I do."

Jec wiggled his big toe. "I'll get a whoopin'."

"Fer goin' out of the house? You jist got through tellin' me you was goin' fishin'." She had caught him lying. He had never lied to her before. "Well, I'm goin' swimmin'. And if you was any kind of friend, Jeconiah Brown, you'd sneak off and go with me." Tessa Mae darted out of the house and ran down towards the woods, making baby chickens scatter this way and that like dandelion fluff.

Soon she slowed down, looked back to see Jec following, and stopped to wait for him. He was carrying a cane fishing pole and a baked bean can filled with dirt and worms.

"It's been a powerful hot day fer May," she said happily. "The swimmin' will be fine."

"I'll sure get a whoopin' if my mama finds out," Jec grumbled.

"Now how's she goin' to find out if you don't tell her? I'm sure not goin' to tell."

A grin spread over Jec's long face. "You some smarter than me, I reckon, Tessa Mae."

The pond, which was bordered by low, rocky cliffs, was still sky colored in the middle, but gray-green shadows scalloped the edges. As a rule Tessa Mae would have slipped out of her blouse and whipped off her gym bloomers, but today something held her back.

"Still think you'll get a whoopin' if you go in?" she asked Jec.

"Yeah, but lookin' at that cool water kinda makes me think it'd be worth it." Jec stared at the pond.

As they stood there together, their thoughts seemed to move towards each other, touch, and exchange some wordless fear. Tessa Mae didn't want to study on what was nagging at both of them, but she knew. It was a part of what had been plaguing her for weeks. There was no name for it, no neat compartment to tuck it into, no place to hide it, although that was what she wanted to do.

They could call off the swimming. She knew it was up to her. But the defiance that had come as companion to the vague uneasiness of the spring overcame her hesitation. Fully clothed, she dived into a deep hole near the rocks, her shorts and blouse constricting her movements. It felt unnatural, but the cool water slid over her like a new day, clean and full of surprises. Surprising the catfish who lived in the pond, she spun around and chased after him, but he flicked his tail and scooted into a hole between two rocks. She sputtered up to the top laughing, and shook her hair to make a mare's tail of water droplets.

Jec cannon-balled into the pond and dog-paddled towards her. "This is real fine, Tessa Mae. I'm glad you talked some sense into me."

"What had you so determined to mind yer mama, Jec? Turnin' over a new leaf?" Tessa Mae noticed that Jec was still wearing his shorts.

"Oh, nothin'. Weren't nothin'. I'll race you."

The pond wasn't large, but they made it seem like one of the big lakes in the geography books by seeing how many circles they could swim without touching down. With six Tessa Mae was way out in front of Jec.

"Whoa," he hollered, then he flopped on the bank like a bass on a line and sucked in air through pursed lips. "I give, Tessa Mae. You outswim any boy I know."

Tessa Mae pulled herself up on a flat rock where the sun filtered through the trees. "I reckon I do, Jec. But I've been swimmin' since I could walk. My daddy jist brought me down here and throwed me in. My mama near lost her voice she screamed so loud."

"Did you near drown?" Jec rolled over, crossed his legs and chewed a plumed weed stem.

"Naw. I paddled around like a puppy. Sure tickled my daddy."

"I don't remember learnin' to swim either. I think I was born knowin' how."

"That ain't possible," Tessa Mae said. "Even ducks have to learn to swim. I've seen 'um. That mother duck pushes them in and they flounder around till they find their paddles." She pulled at her blouse where it stuck to her body like a snake's new skin. What a dumb thing not to have pulled it off. It'd still be wet when she got home, proof that she hadn't been in school. Tessa Mae resolved to worry about that later.

They lay for a while in a peaceful silence, staring up at the awning of hickory leaves that kept the pond cool most of the day even in July and August. Then Tessa Mae sat up, intending to swim one more round before she headed for home. The best thing about her mother going to work had been that she had more freedom. But she knew if she didn't have supper started soon she'd be asked a lot of questions about where she'd been.

"I declare, Tessa Mae." Jec grinned, staring at her chest. "You're getting big. Before you know it, you'll be as big as my mama."

"Lordy, Jec, I hope not." Tessa Mae tried to laugh as she tugged at the wet blouse sticking to her breasts. They *were* getting big, had been since around the time she got her period. At first she'd hoped it was her imagination, but now, with all her shirts and dresses too tight, she knew better.

"Must be a nuisance when they gets to flopping around," Jec said.

"I spec so. Maybe I won't get big enough to flop."

"I'm goin' to get as big as my daddy—all over." Jec grinned.

"Then you'd better get busy growing, Jec. 'Cause you got a ways to go." Tessa Mae laughed again, but she really didn't want to think about getting all grown-up.

"You done it yet with a man?" Jec asked.

"Of course not. What do you take me for? I ain't goin' to neither." Tessa Mae knew all about doing it from the books she'd read. And her imagination had filled in what the books left out.

"Bet you will. Florella did."

"How do you know?" It figured that Florella had done a fool thing like that. Tessa Mae had heard Bertha say over and over that Florella was a misery to her, but she hadn't known exactly what Bertha meant.

"I saw her." Jec grinned again, his white teeth shining like a row of stars. "She's gone plumb nutty over that Abe Pokewith, and they sneaks off together most every night."

"Jec, you got a dirty mind. I'm glad you're not my brother."

"No such luck. You the wrong color," he said back, "and that funny red and yellar hair wouldn't fit in at my house either. Want to know what they was doing?"

"No!" Tessa Mae dived into the cool water, but in a way, she did want to know. It made her feel hot all over thinking about it. She and Florella were the same age, but Florella was much more grown up than Tessa Mae ever wanted to be.

She swam back over to Jec and looked up at him, but didn't get out of the water. For the first time ever, he'd made her feel self-conscious about her body. "You and me ain't never had no secrets from each other, Jec." Tessa Mae grabbed hold of a rock to keep from having to kick her feet. "But yer keepin' one from me now."

"I reckon I got a right to have secrets."

"Since when?"

"Since you started gettin' big, that's when! Mama said she'd whoop me if I went swimmin' with you again. You and me has got too big to play together. What'd you do that fer, Tessa Mae?" Jec started to cry. "Why'd you have to go and get all growed up?"

Tessa Mae stared at him for a minute, then let go of the rock and sank into the cool water. Colder, she knew it had to be colder than this to numb her brain and stop the flurry of thoughts that filled her head.

She kicked her legs together to surface. Then, as her head popped out of the water, she saw Jec standing up. "Get out of there and hide, Tessa Mae," he whispered urgently. "Someone's coming!"

CHAPTER
THREE

Tessa Mae didn't have time to get out of the pond and hide, so she dived beneath the water. When she couldn't hold her breath any longer, she surfaced alongside the big rock, hoping whoever it was would think Jec was alone, fishing.

The intruder was Jec's mother. Bertha had a fishing pole in one hand and was holding on to Jec's ear with the other.

"Jeconiah Brown, what you doin' here? I thought I told you to stay home and help Florella."

Jec wiggled and squirmed as much as he could with Bertha clutching his ear. "I was jist fishin', Mama. Catchin' us a big old catfish for dinner."

Tessa Mae kept only her eyes and nose above water so she could breathe and still see what happened. It looked as if she had gotten Jec in big trouble.

"Look at you, Jec, wet as a drowned rat. You dive in

after that fish? And what makes me think you're not down here fishin' all alone?" Bertha looked around. "Come on out of that pond, Tessa Mae. You ain't foolin' me none by hidin'." Bertha let go of Jec's ear and pushed him towards his fishing pole and bait.

Drowning would have been easier than facing Bertha, but Tessa Mae reluctantly pulled herself out. She started to shiver, only in part because she was cold.

"You get on home, Jec, you hear?" Bertha ordered. "I'll tend to you later. And you tell Florella to get some salt pork and greens cookin'. I'm not goin' to have time to catch us any fish."

Tessa Mae turned to try to make her escape, but it was too late.

"Jist you wait a minute, girl." If Bertha's words hadn't stopped Tessa Mae, her tone of voice would have. Bertha had never called her "girl" like that. "I got some things to say to you."

Bertha's eyes were as black as raven's wings and her face was stormy.

"You tryin' to get my Jec in trouble, Tessa Mae? Big trouble or worse? Is that what yer tryin' to do?"

"Course not, Bertha. Jec's my best friend. Why would I want to hurt Jec?"

Bertha shook her head and leaned back on a rock. "I cain't believe you've lived in this town all yer life and learned nothin' about black folks and white folks. I reckon this is all my fault. I should never have started bringin' Jec over to your house to play. But you didn't have any playmates and Jec was a handful for Florella to look after while I was workin'. I never should have done it." Bertha reached out and pulled Tessa Mae down on the rock beside her. "If you want to be a friend to Jec, Tessa Mae, you'll forget you ever knew him." Bertha's voice had softened.

"Me and Jec cain't be friends no more? We cain't play together?"

"Both of you is gettin' too big to play together, Tessa Mae. Last week Florella told me you two was down here swimmin', naked as the day you was born. Black boys have got themselves killed for less. Much less."

Tessa Mae didn't bother to mention that she was never again going to feel comfortable swimming naked with Jec anyway. It had never entered her mind that she could bring harm to Jec. She knew that some white people hated colored people. But it had been so easy to forget the differences between them. Jec was just her friend.

"It's not fair, Bertha. Jec and me is best friends. I reckon he's jist about my only friend. It's not fair to say we can't be friends anymore, to say I have to forget I ever knew him."

"Fair's got nothin' to do with it. It's not natural for black folks and white folks to be friends."

"Yer my friend, Bertha, and Dee-Dee and Rose Ann and—"

"You'll have to make yourself some new friends now that you're growed up." Bertha got up to leave.

"I'm not growed up! I'm not!" Tessa Mae started to cry. Once she got started, she couldn't stop. It was as if the storm that had been gathering inside of her all spring had cut loose, threatening never to weaken.

Bertha patted her on the shoulder, but Tessa Mae couldn't stop shaking. Finally, when she was able to catch her breath in ragged sobs, she looked up to find that Bertha had gone. She didn't want Bertha to be gone. She wanted Bertha to say that she was angry only because Tessa Mae and Jec had been swimming together without her knowledge, that they could still go fishing together or hunting Indian relics. There was no harm in that, Tessa Mae wanted to say to Bertha. She'd argue until Bertha would say, "Reckon not."

But Bertha was gone and it was getting late. Tessa Mae had to hurry home before her mother got back from work. Now that the vague sense of trouble she'd felt had caught up to her, she had a feeling it wasn't going to stop. Fluffing out her hair, unbuttoning her blouse to flap it in the breeze, she ran down the path towards home. Later, if her mother asked, she would say she'd been washing her hair. But Tessa Mae had run out of luck for the day. Just as she reached the house her mother stepped from the kitchen out onto the screened-in sleeping porch.

"Where've you been, Tessa Mae?" Her mother placed her hands on her hips. "I don't like comin' home to an empty house. Not that I expected Roy Glen to be here, but you was supposed to have supper started. Do you know what time it is? It's nearly six o'clock."

"I've been walkin'." Tessa Mae eased the door closed but stayed close to it in case she needed to escape. She had learned that the less she said to her mother, the better.

"You haven't jist been walkin'. Yer hair and yer clothes are wet. And Dixie Lee come in from lunch and said she seen you headin' over towards Elbert and Maudie's. Did you skip school?"

"We had a teachers' meetin' this afternoon."

"Then why was all the rest of the school goin' home at three-thirty like usual? I'm tired of you lyin' to me, Tessa Mae."

And I'm tired of your asking me questions I have to lie about, thought Tessa Mae.

"Have you been swimmin' with Jec?"

Tessa Mae, ignoring her damp clothes, eased into the

kitchen to peel the potatoes for supper, concentrating on the knife to make it move under the skin so it came off real thin like her mother liked. She didn't want to get yelled at for peeling potatoes wrong, too.

Her mother followed her into the kitchen and repeated, "I asked if you been swimmin' with Jeconiah," then stood grimly waiting for an answer. Finally, she said, "Don't bother to lie to me again, Tessa Mae. After Florella told Bertha what you been up to, Bertha came straight to me, worried sick. I knew you wouldn't mind me, so I told her to try to git it stopped from that end."

She turned to the stove. "I might of known you'd go hog wild when I had to go to work."

Tessa Mae leaped at the chance to change the subject. "I thought you went to work because you wanted to, Mama, not because you had to."

"I wanted to know some money was coming in here regular." The smell of frying pork chops filled the big kitchen.

"Daddy brings in plenty of money." Tessa Mae chopped the potatoes in small pieces for frying.

"Not regular. I never know if we're goin' to have a penny from day to day. What extra he has, he spends on liquor."

Her mother was always pestering Roy Glen about money. Tessa Mae herself believed that money was like time. There was always plenty if you didn't worry about it.

Tessa Mae put the potatoes into a skillet of bacon grease to fry, then fled to her room and shucked off her damp clothes. Searching through her closet, she realized she'd left her dress and shoes under the bush in the woods.

Clothes were getting to be a problem since she'd begun to grow so fast. She could still wear a couple of her dresses, but the only jeans that fit her had a worn-out knee. She chose a cotton dress, faded like the calico, and her old scuffs.

Then she ran a comb through her hair, pulling out the tangles. When she was done it still looked like unraveled rope, so she took time to weave it into one braid down her back.

Tessa Mae stayed in her bedroom waiting for Roy Glen to come in. When she heard his voice, she went back out to the kitchen.

Her daddy was sitting at the table, his newspaper spread out before him. He winked at Tessa Mae and she smiled, then hurried to the silverware drawer.

"Roy Glen"—her mama wasn't about to let up—"you tell this child she's too old to keep on runnin' with that Jeconiah Brown."

"If I'm a child, then I'm not too old."

"You hush your mouth, Tessa Mae Ferris. I'm talkin' to your daddy."

"I don't see no harm in it, Vinnie." Roy Glen didn't look up from his newspaper. "They was raised together. And since you didn't see fit to give her no brothers or sisters to play with—"

"Now, don't go waggin' that tail again, Roy Glen. You know the doctor said I was too frail to have another child."

Tessa Mae thought her mama looked about as frail as Jec's old cow, Juno. She was taller than most women Tessa Mae'd seen, and big boned. Her hands, reddened by her laundry work, pushed the biscuit dough around as if it were a wad of chewing gum. She probably had been pretty once, but now she was starting to look worn down. Tessa Mae still hadn't figured out why her mother had gone to work at the laundry.

As if she were changing the subject quickly, her mother started on her second favorite complaint, after Tessa Mae's behavior. "That store next to Stubblefield's Merchantile is comin' up fer rent again, Roy Glen. I think it'd be a good idea to—"

"I don't want to open no store, Vinnie. How many times do I have to tell you that? Besides, what would I sell in a store? Nails and screws and light bulbs?"

Tessa Mae glanced at her daddy who had folded up the newspaper as he and her mother talked. His long fingers began playing with the silverware Tessa Mae had put in front of him. She tried to picture her daddy in a store, but she couldn't. Didn't her mother realize that it would be like trapping a bird in a cage to put Roy Glen behind a counter?

It seemed to Tessa Mae that her mother had taken to complaining more and more since she went to work. She guessed that her mother was so tired at night, she was taking it out on them. Or maybe with summer coming, she had renewed hope that they'd move into town and change the life she never seemed satisfied with. Sometimes Tessa Mae wished for once Roy Glen would stand up to Mama and argue back, even though that wasn't his way. Roy Glen would close up within himself, or go off to his work space and stay out of sight. His way was the same as Tessa Mae's, and maybe that's where she got the habit of running off. Tessa Mae figured her daddy wished he could escape now, but with biscuits in the oven and pork chops frying he'd stay put.

Her mother had an answer ready about merchandise for the store. "Maybe you could sell some of that junk that's stacked in the bedroom and out in the shed. If people's dumb enough to order it by mail, they'd surely buy it in a store." As she spoke she turned the potatoes, while she poured water into the pork chops, leaving them to simmer.

"The people who mail-order Indian relics don't pass through downtown Lamar, Vinnie. They don't even come through downtown Little Rock, or any other place in Arkansas."

"Well, at least it'd look like you was workin'." Mama's voice continued to harp bitterly about other people's opinion of the Ferrises.

Tessa Mae sat staring at the table. As far as she was concerned, the way they lived was nobody else's business. The seventh-grade kids had thought she was odd when she didn't start dressing in fancy, store-bought clothes and making cow eyes at all the boys she'd played ball with the year before. But it didn't make her want to be like them. Her daddy couldn't be like the other men in Lamar, going to work every day at eight o'clock, getting home at five-fifteen, any more than she could be like Erline Crider.

Her mother was still talking on and on, so Tessa Mae broke in, trying to change the subject. She knew that Roy Glen must hate her mother's nagging at him all the time as much as she did.

"My dresses are all too tight, Mama. Can't I get me a pair of shorts tomorrow fer summer? I could find some nice ones, and a shirt too, fer about two dollars."

"That's another reason why you should stay away from that boy, Jeconiah, Tessa Mae. And any other boys." Her mother started to dish up the food while Tessa Mae got up and poured iced tea.

" 'Cause I need some shorts?" Tessa Mae pretended not to know what her mother meant.

"Your dresses are too tight, young lady, because your figure is developin'. And girls who are developin' have no business messin' around in the woods with boys, black or white." Her mama made it sound like some kind of disease—*developing*.

Tessa Mae got up and poured Roy Glen some coffee, then passed him the biscuits. It was a fine supper, but no one was enjoying it.

"We was jist swimmin', Mama. No harm in swimmin'."

"There is too. Especially if you got yer clothes off. That's jist how it all starts."

"How what starts?" Tessa Mae thought she might as well get her mama going good now that she'd brought up the subject.

"Don't try and act so innocent, Tessa Mae. You know exactly what I'm talkin' about."

" 'Peers she might not, Vinnie. What have you told her?" Roy Glen buttered a biscuit and looked at Tessa Mae. She loved the way his gray eyes said, "I love you, baby, but you shouldn't have riled your mama like this."

"You two!" Mama shook her head. "Not everybody ignores the real world like you do, Roy Glen."

"Might be better off if they did." He sipped his coffee, his long, thin fingers circling the brown cup.

Sensitive fingers, a poet would call them. Tessa Mae had read a poem last week that talked about a master potter with sensitive hands who shaped the people around him like he'd shape clay. Her daddy had done a lot to shape her life whether he knew it or not.

Knowing Tessa Mae took after her daddy probably made her mother the maddest. Maybe, she imagined, when a woman went to all the trouble to have a baby girl, she'd expect it to be more like her.

"The boys aren't going to ignore Tessa Mae's developin' figure, Roy Glen. You can count on it. First thing you know Tessa Mae will be in trouble. Look at Florella Brown, pregnant and givin' Bertha all that misery. You can't let a girl Tessa Mae's age run loose in the woods."

"Maybe she needs her mama home to look after her." Roy Glen rolled himself a cigarette.

"That's right, blame it on me. Yer the one who encourages her to go off down there in the woods." Suddenly Mama burst out crying. "I cain't take much more of either one of you," she sobbed and ran from the kitchen.

Tessa Mae stacked the dishes together and carried them to the sink. "I don't hardly ever remember seeing Mama cry," she told Roy Glen. "I guess we made her madder than usual."

"I reckon so." Roy Glen got up and headed out to the shed off to the side of the house that he used as an office.

In the evenings, Roy Glen would sort through the mail orders for the pots and arrowheads and other Indian relics he dug out of the river bottoms and fields. Often he let Tessa Mae open the letters and separate the orders and the checks. It seemed a wonder to her that a person in Illinois or California would want something that was dug up in Arkansas.

The orders never stopped coming, even during the war, but Roy Glen predicted that 1946 was going to be his best year yet, because people had money again, and they weren't afraid to spend it. The Ferrises sure weren't rich, but Tessa Mae thought the way the mail was running they might be soon.

If her mother took an interest in Roy Glen's business, she'd see that too. But Mama never went out to the office unless she had to because it was too dirty and piled up for her taste. There was an order to it if a person took time to see it. But Mama never took time to do anything but complain.

Tessa Mae had poured hot water from the tea kettle into the sink, waited for the soap to foam up, then began on the glasses and cups. The last dish wiped and put away, she tiptoed through the living room and stood in front of her parents' bedroom. The room seemed quiet and no light shone from beneath the door. Maybe her mother had already gone to bed. She had to be at the laundry at seven o'clock, even on Saturday.

Slipping out the back door, Tessa Mae stopped for a minute to sniff the lilacs blooming out along the back fence. A mockingbird was talking about how it was time for everyone to get ready for the night. Whip-poor-wills in the woods behind the house celebrated the setting sun as Tessa Mae picked her way to Roy Glen's shed.

He was sitting at his desk, with his back to her. Piles of letters, books, and magazines spilled over the top of the desk and onto the floor. It wasn't hard to see why her mother thought the office was a mess.

Roy Glen didn't have a chance to get the liquor bottle put away before Tessa Mae saw it. She knew he took a drink once in a while, especially in the evening, but that was all right with her. In some books, rich people had wine with their dinner every night. And in the Bible even poor people drank wine. Once when they ran out of refreshments at a big wedding party Jesus helped them by turning some of the water they had into more wine. If drinking was wrong, Tessa Mae figured it wouldn't be in the Bible.

She knew her daddy couldn't be spending all his money on liquor either, because he always seemed to have plenty. Nearly every week he'd put some change in her hand or her pocket when her mother wasn't looking. Before long he'd give her two dollars for the shorts.

"Kin I help you out, Roy Glen? I don't have no lessons or anything new to read."

"I don't need no help tonight, Baby. Go check and see if your mama is okay."

"I did that. I reckon she's already gone to bed. It's quiet in there."

Tessa Mae wavered uncertainly in the doorway. Roy Glen

didn't seem to want to talk. He didn't encourage her to hang around. Maybe, because he and her mama were fighting, he'd had more to drink than usual. He got even quieter when he'd been drinking.

She turned and walked back through the darkness, then sank down on the steps. The sweet smell of Mama's climbing yellow roses filled the air, sickening her. The world Tessa Mae had always known, always depended on to form a safe, warm cocoon around her seemed as far away as the pinpoints of light appearing in the black velvet sky.

She tried to find the familiar magic in the late spring evening, the anticipation of the summer to come. But she couldn't. As she hugged her knees tight up under her chin, making herself as small as she felt, Tessa Mae knew a part of her life had slipped away from her that very day. Never again was she going to experience the long summer days spent chasing Jec through the woods. Never again would she feel as free as the animals who wandered to the river to drink. And already her mother's laughter at Roy Glen's stories seemed a memory.

A dove's song floated mournfully across the night air, echoing through the hollow spaces the realization left inside her.

CHAPTER
FOUR

Saturday mornings Tessa Mae was allowed to lie in bed as late as she wanted, but this particular Saturday she couldn't go back to sleep. A cardinal had awakened her, calling, *What cheer, what cheer?* "No cheer, no cheer," she grumbled. "No cheer at all."

After yesterday, there wasn't a whole lot to get up for. She couldn't wander down to Jec's and go swimming. Fishing wasn't always a lot of fun alone. There was always the woods but that just didn't appeal to her enough to move. Finally she decided she was hungry.

She dressed quickly, in a shirt and her gym bloomers, knowing she'd have to wash the bloomers over the weekend or get a demerit on Monday.

There was a note from her mother in the kitchen. "After breakfast I need for you to do the ironing. Bertha can't come this week."

It struck Tessa Mae as funny that her mother was work-ing washing someone else's laundry but still hired Bertha to do theirs. Tessa Mae wondered why Bertha couldn't come. Maybe she had her hands full with Florella's trouble this morning. Or maybe she was so angry at Tessa Mae that she was never going to work for them again.

Ironing was usually a good time for thinking, but today Tessa Mae didn't want to think. She put her mind on smoothing the wrinkles out of Roy Glen's shirts and her mother's dresses. The starch smell was sweet and the car-dinal now joined by a robin chorus, was still singing. She dug in the pillow case of damp clothes, keeping her mind on nothing.

When she finished up the last blouse and put the iron aside to cool, she stirred up a glass of iced tea with lemon and sugar the way she liked it. Then she went and sat in a rocker on the sleeping porch and moved the air around with a Greenwood Mortuary fan. The picture on the paste-board give-away was a white farmhouse with big trees and blooming flowers all around it. A lady in a white dress sat in a lawn chair. The shady yard was supposed to make her feel cool, she guessed, but today it didn't help much.

Tessa Mae's shoulders ached and the sweat trickled down between her breasts, wetting her shirt to the waist. She longed to jump up and run all the way to the swimming pond, but she stayed where she was and kept rocking. Just about the time she'd decided to go see if Roy Glen was home and ask him if he wanted a sandwich, her mother walked up the back steps.

"What are you doin' home so early, Mama?" Tessa Mae stopped rocking and put down the fan. "Is anythin' wrong?" Maybe her mother had quit her job, she thought. Maybe she had decided she was too tired at night and too grouchy all the time, and that the job wasn't worth her feeling that

way. Maybe she'd said, "I don't need yer old job. My husband makes plenty of money, and I was jist workin' fer
fun."

But Mama didn't have on her laundry clothes. She was
wearing her best Sunday dress, the new one she'd got for
Easter.

"Where've you been, Mama?" Tessa Mae saw that her
mother looked pale. "Want me to fix you a glass of iced
tea?"

"That'd be nice, Tessa Mae." Her mother sat in the other
rocker while Tessa Mae hurried out into the kitchen to get
the tea. She squeezed in lemon and put in an extra spoon
of sugar, hoping that would make her mother feel better.

"Thank you, Tessa Mae." Her mother sipped the cool
drink and took a deep breath. "Sit back down here. I need
to talk to you."

Suddenly Tessa Mae felt scared. For two or three weeks
Mama had been as nervous as a rabbit in a snake's sights.
But now, she just seemed worn out.

"I've been talkin' to the Reverend Mr. Peterson, and then
I went to see a lawyer. I've made up my mind at last. Yer
daddy's drinkin' and no-account ways has finally worn me
down. I'm goin' to leave him, and then I'm goin' to get me
a divorce. We're movin' to town."

"We?" Tessa Mae stared at the pattern of sweat beads
on her iced tea glass. A divorce? She didn't know anyone
whose mama and daddy had gotten a divorce. Divorce happened in some of the stories she read, but not in a little
town like Lamar. She decided that her mother had got a
good case of heat stroke from walking from town at midday.

"You and me are goin' to live in that little house back of
Ruby Gilliard's Beauty Shop. Her renter moved out and I
was able to get it jist this mornin' after I talked to the

Reverend Mr. Peterson. It's got two bedrooms, so you kin still have your own room. You kin get a part-time job, and by fall you'll have a lot of pretty clothes to wear to ninth grade. You kin even walk to school, too, and stop ridin' that school bus with all those nigra children and poor white trash from down on the river bottoms."

"I don't mind riding the school bus, Mama."

"But going to ninth grade, Tessa Mae, you'll want to bring yer friends home and have sleepin'-over parties, and there's dances and basketball games . . ."

It didn't seem like a good time to tell Mama that she didn't have any friends who would want to spend the night— here *or* in the little house behind Ruby Gilliard's Beauty Shop. Except Jec. But if he couldn't go swimming with her, he sure couldn't spend the night. The very idea of asking her mother if Jec could sleep over made her giggle.

Her mother smiled. "See, I knew you'd like the idea. I'm doin' this for both of us. We're goin' to have a lot of fun in town. Now you get busy packin'. I left some boxes by the steps. Reverend Peterson has kindly offered to come and get us about five o'clock this afternoon. I'm going to tell yer daddy if he isn't too drunk to listen."

Roy Glen wouldn't be drunk. He'd be working. But Tessa Mae didn't tell her mother that. She didn't tell her anything. She didn't say anything, because she didn't know what to say. She couldn't even think. She just sat there, rocking and fanning herself while her mother went out towards the shed.

Tessa Mae finally came to her senses. It isn't fair, she thought. It wasn't fair for her mother to just walk in and tell her they were moving out, leaving Roy Glen here alone. Well, she wasn't going.

Tessa Mae ran out the back door, letting the screen slam

behind her. Out behind the house was a garage with sagging doors and peeling paint, which was mostly full of junk. Roy Glen's 1936 Dodge panel truck sat in the driveway. Tessa Mae skirted it and headed for the grape arbor beside the garage.

The grape arbor had been Tessa Mae's special place since she was a little girl. Over the years the vines had grown to leave space for her, and she had a hollowed-out room up beside the garage wall. She loved crawling in under the cool, green leaves to her personal, private thinking place, her reading place, her hiding-from-the-world place. Right then she wanted to crawl in there and stay forever, because her mother was doing some plumb crazy thing and was trying to make Tessa Mae do it with her.

And what about Roy Glen? Tessa Mae didn't want to leave him even if her mama did. She decided right then to stay and live with him. He'd need someone to cook for him and iron his shirts, help him with his orders. Those were things she'd be glad to do. Then her mother could be rid of them both. After all, she'd said she was sick of them. She could live in town and do the things she thought were fun. She could have all the pretty dresses she wanted.

Fuming, Tessa Mae pressed hard against the garage wall. Mama didn't have any right to call Roy Glen a drunk, either. Sure, he could get a little carried away, like he had last night after the fight. But normally he drank only when the weather stayed bad for days, or the orders weren't coming in. She had never seen him drunk like Mr. Groober, who hung out down at Billy Ray Joiner's pool hall. Early one Sunday morning Tessa Mae and her mother had to walk around him because he was sleeping on the sidewalk. Mama had said drinking was a sin and that the devil had a good hold on old man Groober.

Wasn't divorce a sin, too? Tessa Mae wondered. It must be, because nobody ever did it. She tried to remember what the Bible said about divorce, but she couldn't. Her mother said she'd talked to the Reverend Mr. Peterson, and he surely would have told Mama if divorce was a sin. The Reverend Mr. Peterson was an authority on sinning.

Mr. Inky smiled and Tessa Mae realized she'd been talking out loud. Mr. Inky was a black snake that lived in the grape arbor, and he'd been Tessa Mae's friend for she couldn't remember how long. Most people would be surprised to learn that a snake could smile, but when you've known a snake as long as she'd known Mr. Inky, you could tell a smile when you see one. Mr. Inky wove his shiny body around a brown, peeling vine and slid on down to the ground. It soothed her to know that part of the world was still natural and the same.

Her mother's voice cut into the peace and quiet she had managed to find, shattering it again. "Tessa Mae, you get out of there, you hear? I know yer in that grape arbor. I told you to pack your things. I told Roy Glen we was goin', and he said, fine, get out. So you hurry up. I don't want the Reverend Peterson to have to wait on us."

Tessa Mae knew her daddy couldn't have said that their leaving was fine. He probably hadn't said anything. Maybe he thought he'd be plumb glad to get rid of her mama's nagging all the time, but she knew he hadn't said that either. He probably had kept on working without even looking up.

She couldn't worry about Roy Glen right now, though. The big question was what could *she* do?

Hearing the door slam at last, Tessa Mae crawled out of the cool tangle of vines and slipped along behind the garage to the shed where her daddy was working. She wanted to hear for herself how he felt about them leaving. Then she'd tell him she intended to stay there with him, and they'd both stand up against Mama together.

But Roy Glen was gone. Tessa Mae looked around the piles of dusty magazines, boxes of grinding stones and arrowheads, and down the aisles of pottery and some Indian blankets he'd gotten in a trade. Half a cup of cold coffee and a saucer of stubbed-out cigarettes said he'd worked there at his desk all morning. An empty bottle of Old Crow lay on its side halfway under the desk, but Tessa Mae didn't let her eyes rest on it. She checked the wooden box beside the back door. His bedroll and some tools were gone. He'd headed for a dig, she realized, packed up in a hurry and run off, leaving her to deal with her mother by herself.

The old Dodge still squatted in the driveway, so she knew he'd gone on foot. She hesitated a moment, her hand on the sun-warmed hood of the truck. She could find him easily enough. She knew all his places. There was a site down on the river about two miles from home, and the other, closer site, where she'd found him yesterday. Her bedroll was in the house, and she was still barefoot. If she was going after Roy Glen, she'd need her shoes. The paths to the second river camp got wilder, and there'd be plenty of snakes.

Slowly she picked up a box near the back steps and slammed the door as she headed for her room.

"Just take some clothes and things you'll need for school next week. We'll come back and get the rest gradual like," her mama called.

Tessa Mae threw some things into the box, all the while sorting out another pile. She took her one pair of jeans, with the worn-through knee, and tossed them into the old army blanket she kept for camping. Later, she'd cut them off for shorts. Then she added two shirts, a jacket, an extra pair of socks and underwear, and the knife her daddy had given her for Christmas last year. She made sure her mother was busy in her closet and made a silent trip into the kitchen for a box of Ritz crackers, a hunk of bologna, and two apples and a banana. She tossed the food onto the blanket, then remembered her notebook under the mattress. She lifted the corner, snatched it out, folded over two ends of the blanket, and rolled the whole pack up. Hearing her mother coming, she kicked it under the bed just in time.

"There's beds in that house but no linens," said her mother, standing in the doorway. "So take yer extra pair of sheets and fold them into the box. Take yer pillow and yer spread, too." She looked excited, her cheeks flushed and her hair tousled. "I cain't believe we're finally goin' to live in town instead of way out here in the sticks. Get busy, Tessa Mae. You've hardly started packin'." She disappeared through the living room and back into her bedroom.

Now was Tessa Mae's chance. She grabbed the blanket from under the bed, wadded it together, and headed for the back door. Making sure the screen didn't slam, she took off running through the yard to Roy Glen's shed. She measured off a length of heavy twine and snipped it loose, wrapping it around her fist. Back outside, she raced down the path to the woods, not looking back.

By the time she'd got to the hydrangea bush where her shoes were hidden, she decided to stop. First she tied up her blanket of supplies like a Christmas package. Then she squeezed on her shoes. They were getting too tight, but she could always cut out the toes for the rare times she'd have to wear them. She left her school dress hanging on a hickory limb like a freedom flag, and set off down the pathway.

It was cooler by the river. Only a few late dogwood trees

still wore their tiny green blossoms and white petal-like leaves, but the dogwood fragrance still seemed to linger. Perhaps it was stored in her memory. The ground around the wild plum trees was littered with petals that dropped like snowflakes.

Spring had come late, but now it was almost over as the heat of May gained strength. Ferns had started to unfold in the boggy places where streams fed the river, and in the shade a few wood violets continued to bloom. Tessa Mae couldn't walk quietly in her shoes, and a brown thrasher took flight when she broke a twig on the path.

"Sorry," she said, and laughed as he lit and looked at her with his big yellow eyes.

Roy Glen wasn't at the Friday place. He'd most likely gone off farther, as far away as he could from her mother's fool idea. After a couple of miles she was hot and dusty, but the inside of her head felt better. She hurried on, hoping she was right about Roy Glen's whereabouts.

Sure enough, Roy Glen had come to the far river camp. As she neared a small clearing, she saw his bedroll tossed against a log, and a shovel stood where he had planted it in the soft ground. He slumped, head down on his chest, on a rock beside a long dead fire.

"Roy Glen," she called out, running the last few steps. "I knew you'd be here."

He looked up. "What are you doin' here, Tessa Mae?" he said in a husky voice. "You belong with your mother. Get on back home and move to town with her."

CHAPTER
FIVE

Move to town with Mama? Her daddy's words made Tessa Mae feel as empty as one of the old red wolves that worked the river bottoms alone. She'd seen them, hunting without the strength of the pack—no mate, no partner—settling for anything they could catch by themselves to eat.

Roy Glen looked as if he'd been crying. His voice was thick and husky, and it appeared that "go home" was all he was going to say.

Tessa Mae sat on the log and waited while the silence got louder. A fly buzzed close by her and she sent it on. A mosquito whined at her ear and she waved it away. The brown thrasher's call rang out across the sluggish river, which ran wide and slowed down at this point even with the spring rains.

Tessa Mae couldn't wait forever. "Mama kin move to

town by herself, Roy Glen," she said at last. "I won't go. I want to stay here with you."

Roy Glen raised his head and looked beyond Tessa Mae as if she wasn't there, as if he was alone with the Indian ghosts from the past. His eyes were red-rimmed, his dark hair fell into his face instead of being swept back like he usually wore it.

With shaking hands he took a pack of Camels from his shirt pocket. He scratched a match with his thumbnail, cupped his hands around the flame, and lit the cigarette. After a long drag he held it between tobacco-stained fingers and said, "You cain't stay here with me. I cain't take care of you."

"But I'll take care of you, Daddy. I'm big now—fourteen—remember? I kin cook and iron, and I'll help you with your diggin' and your mail orders. We'll do just fine."

"You have to go to school."

"You didn't finish school. I don't need to either. I kin read books, and you kin teach me more than them old schoolteachers know anyway."

Tessa Mae knew Roy Glen had gone only through the seventh grade. She could get all her school books and read them like he had done when he was a boy. All the teachers ever did was talk about what was in the books anyway. They didn't tell her anything new.

"I want you to go to town, Tessa Mae. I don't want you livin' here with me. Now go along. You kin catch your mother before she leaves." He ground out his cigarette under the heel of his boot and stared at the ground.

Tessa Mae tried to catch his gaze. If he'd look at her, maybe she could tell if he was lying. But his eyes had gone off again, staring at nothing.

"Are you drunk, Daddy?" If he was drunk, maybe he didn't know what he was saying.

"No, I'm not drunk, Tessa Mae. Jist leave me alone."

The words fell heavily into the quiet of the clearing. But Tessa Mae couldn't leave, not without having something to hold on to, something for later if not for today. "If I go into town with Mama, kin I come and visit you anytime I want to? Camp out with you? Go diggin' when you find a new site?"

"I don't know, Tessa Mae. We'll see what your mama says."

What Mama says, always what Mama says! Tessa Mae clenched her fists and bit her tongue to keep from shouting the words. If Roy Glen wanted to confront her mama, see what she'd say, they could go back together right now. She'd stand beside him while he said, "I want Tessa Mae to come and live with me, not go live in town." She'd say, "I'm old enough to decide where to live, Mama." And faced with both of them Mama would give up.

But it seemed that it was Roy Glen who had given up. Sprawled on the ground and looking defeated, he was obviously not about to go anywhere. Tessa Mae would have to make her own decision.

Stumbling, she got to her feet and yanked on the blanket-roll pack. The scratchy wool bumped into her arms, and she let the tears drop onto the dark brown cloth. She turned and started back the way she'd come. Then, once more, she looked back at her daddy. His elbows rested on his knees and his head was in his hands.

"Bye, Daddy. You take care of yerself, hear? I'll come back later. I won't ask Mama. I'll decide fer myself."

He appeared not to hear her. She made a lot of noise on the path, to attract his attention, but she only scared a king snake that slithered away as fast as he could move. Roy Glen didn't call out, "Come back, Tessa Mae. I've changed my mind." He didn't call out anything at all.

As she retraced her steps, Tessa Mae's frustration turned to anger. For the first time in her life, she felt truly helpless. It wasn't in her nature to be helpless. Roy Glen loved telling about the time when she started to walk, how she'd slap anyone's hand that reached out to her. She'd say, "No," when he or her mama tried to help her up when she fell. "Myself" had been her favorite word. Later she added, "Do it myself." She had always accepted Roy Glen's laughter when she said it as an encouragement for her independence. But now it appeared that Mama was going to be able to tell her what to do. Mama'd won. She always won.

Coming into the yard, Tessa Mae saw a shiny new Ford parked behind the Dodge panel truck. The Reverend Peterson in his shirtsleeves stood with his foot on the running board, talking to her mother.

"Here she is now, Reverend Peterson. I told you she'd be ready in a jiffy. She jist went to get the rest of her things. Put that in the trunk, Tessa Mae, and we'll be all ready to go. We don't want to keep Reverend Peterson from his dinner."

Tessa Mae figured that no one kept the Reverend Peterson from his dinner very often. He wasn't old, but his stomach bulged out from his light blue trousers and his face was all pink and flushed from the heat. He reached out pudgy fingers for Tessa Mae's bedroll, but she jerked it back and placed it in the trunk herself. Her mother must have finished packing since there were two boxes filled to the top. Their old brown suitcase was wedged between them. Tessa Mae shoved her pack on top of the suitcase and way back so the trunk would close.

Without saying a word, she got in the back seat and rolled down her window. Mama chattered on and on, while they bumped along to town, about how they could finally go to church socials and movies and Tessa Mae would have a place to entertain her friends. Tessa Mae bit her lower lip to keep from speaking out. They hadn't lived so far from town that she couldn't go to the picture show, and Mama went to the church parties when she wanted to. Those were just excuses for leaving Roy Glen.

"I really appreciate yer help, Reverend Peterson," Mama said.

"Glad to oblige, Vinnie. I know how hard this must be for you." A big diamond sparkled on the Reverend's finger as he spun the steering wheel.

"Yes. Yes, it is. But I've made up my mind. I cain't take no more of that man's good-for-nothin' ways. This move is goin' to be best for me and Tessa Mae, too. She's goin' to be in ninth grade next year."

"That's real fine, Tessa Mae. Yer growing up, aren't you?"

"She sure is." Her mother answered for Tessa Mae. "Why she might even go to the college over in Russellville. She's a real smart girl."

So Mama intended to keep deciding what was best for her. She was even telling Reverend Peterson what Tessa Mae was going to do when she grew up. And Tessa Mae had no choice but to go along, trapped in the preacher's car as they came into Lamar, away from everything she cared about.

The town of Lamar consisted of a few stores and a post office on Main Street. Two streets over was a peach shed belonging to J. H. Hamilton's orchard. Folks said that J. H. Hamilton was so rich he had money enough to burn a wet mule. The peach orchard wasn't operating in May, of course, since peaches come ripe in August. Tessa Mae thought about getting a job in the peach shed. Maybe she could save enough money to get herself a tent and go off and live alone like that fellow Thoreau.

Train tracks ran right through town, and a sign at the

depot announced, Lamar, Population 683. Old men sat on the benches in front of the depot despite the fact that the only train from Little Rock had come and gone at noon.

Ruby Gilliard's Beauty Shop was on the edge of the residential section. Houses here were in sharp contrast to the homes east of the elementary and junior high schools where Erline Crider and Sue Anne Sparks lived. The church was close by, but the high school was out on the highway, and students were bused in from all the little farming communities around Lamar.

Ruby Gilliard had moved to the rooms over her shop and rented the little house at the back after her husband had died in the war. She and Tessa Mae's mother were only "speaking" friends, since neither of them had much time to visit.

The Reverend Peterson stopped in the driveway behind the shop and helped carry in the boxes. Tessa Mae carried in the old suitcase and her bedroll.

"Ain't this nice, Tessa Mae?" her mother said, looking around.

If her mother was aiming to better herself, this house wasn't much of a step up from where they'd lived in the woods. It had four rooms and an indoor bathroom. Tessa Mae supposed city water came from the tap in the kitchen like it did at school, but it wouldn't taste as good as their well water. The living room windows had beige curtains with yellow chrysanthemums. There was a brown couch and two olive green chairs perching on a worn, muddy-colored carpet. On the wall behind the couch was a big picture of a purple mountain and some clouds and sheep. It was hard to tell the difference between the clouds and the sheep, except the clouds were in the sky and the sheep on the green grass. Behind one chair was a picture of Jesus when he was a boy.

Her mother steered Tessa Mae into the room on the right of the bathroom. "Put that box in here please, Reverend Peterson. This is Tessa Mae's room. And we do thank you again."

There was a single bed with a gray-striped mattress on it. A small table and chair sat in front of the window, decorated at the moment by a vase of artificial flowers left by some long-departed renter. The wallpaper was splashed with big, blotchy pink roses. Tessa Mae sat down on the bed and kicked at her bedroll, which slumped on the pink and green linoleum like a good-for-nothing old hound dog.

This was her new home. This was where she was supposed to invite all her friends for after-school cold drinks and slumber parties. She could just see Erline Crider sitting there at the table in a pink dotted Swiss dress saying, "This is real fine, Tessa Mae. I'm so glad you invited me over."

A truck rattled down the road, breaking the silence. Two boys on the sidewalk hollered at the man in the truck and he honked his horn. Tessa Mae could see right past the beauty shop and into the street. She guessed she would have to pull the roller shade at night.

"I was so embarrassed in front of the Reverend Peterson, Tessa Mae." Her mama stood in the doorway, hands on her hips. "How could you run away like that? You should have known it wouldn't do any good. I hope yer satisfied. I'm goin' to forget the way you acted, though. We'll put all that behind us and start our new life. I'll bring yer curtains from home and some rugs and a lamp for beside yer bed. Now you get to work unpackin' yer clothes and then change into a dress. We'll go over to the cafe and get us some dinner. Won't that be a treat?"

Automatically Tessa Mae obeyed her mother. Pushing aside a curtain, which served as the closet door, she hung up the few clothes her mother had packed. Hadn't Mama noticed that she couldn't wear most of these dresses because she was growing up? If moving into this house, getting a summer job, was really what growing up meant, it confirmed Tessa Mae's feeling that she didn't want any part of it. She didn't want to go to high school, and certainly she had no plan for college.

She pushed hangers this way and that until she found a red-and-white seersucker dress that was designed to hang loose. Her mother had ordered it from the Sears catalogue for Sunday best. She had never liked it much, but she put it on, laced her shoes back up after putting on clean socks, and folded her sock tops over neatly.

Sitting on the bed, she focused on the dusty, crepe paper roses and waited for her mother to tell her what to do next.

CHAPTER
SIX

She wore the same dress Sunday morning and sat through Sunday School and church without speaking to anyone. She hoped no one had noticed that she and her mother had walked up to the church yard from a different direction than usual. Her daddy's not being along raised no eyebrows. Roy Glen had never gone to church with them; and since Tessa Mae's mother didn't drive, they always walked to town for the service. Tessa Mae wanted to keep her new living arrangement secret as long as possible. If people thought she was strange before, she and her mother moving to town without Roy Glen was going to intensify their idea.

When Reverend Peterson announced the song before the sermon Tessa Mae turned her hymn book to the page.

"How firm a foundation, ye saints of the Lord," she started to sing, because this was one of her favorites. But she couldn't concentrate on the music for thinking about her own shaky foundation. She put the hymnal away and turned to her Bible, paging through it to see if she could find anything to help her with her trouble. She found passage after passage about money, but not a mention of divorce. It seemed as if having too much money was the bigger sin by far. Or maybe, Tessa Mae reflected, people didn't divorce in Bible times either, so Jesus never got around to saying anything about it.

In the "thou shalt nots" there was mention of adultery. Tessa Mae was twelve before she found out that adultery meant running off with someone else's husband or wife. Even then she had to ask Jec. As far as she knew, her mother hadn't committed adultery. Tessa Mae sat back in the pew. It was possible Mama might still have God on her side, divorce and all.

When the last amen was said and echoed by the congregation, people streamed out of the church and stood in groups on the lawn, visiting.

Tessa Mae's mother stopped to speak to Dixie Lee Tooley. Dixie Lee was younger than her mama and didn't have any kids. Her husband, a truck driver, was often gone for a night or more when he had a long haul. Mr. Tooley had bought a pick-up truck when he came home from the war and sometimes Dixie Lee drove it out to see Tessa Mae and her mama on a Sunday afternoon when her husband was gone.

Dixie Lee put her arm around Tessa Mae's mother as they walked towards town. "It was such a nice day I decided I'd walk to church instead of drivin' that big old truck. How're you doin', Vinnie? You all right?"

Tessa Mae stopped listening. Why shouldn't Mama be all right? After all, the whole thing was her idea. Why didn't Dixie Lee ask Tessa Mae if *she* was okay?

When they got close to the little rented house Tessa Mae's mother said, "Come on, Tessa Mae. We're goin' home with Dixie Lee fer lunch. She's feelin' sorry fer us because we have to eat at the cafe, and I was thinkin' what a treat it was."

Dinner the previous night at the cafe hadn't been that much of a treat. They'd had chicken that was so tough you couldn't stick a fork in the gravy. And the corn bread was sweet and crumbly instead of salty and chewy like Bertha's. Although Tessa Mae didn't want to go home with Dixie Lee, her stomach had been rumbling since the offering plate went around. All they'd had for breakfast was a package of store-bought doughnuts and a cup of coffee. Mama hadn't had time to get groceries into the new place, but if they kept eating at the cafe, people would start wondering why they were there instead of at home. It was funny that her Mama, who cared so much what other people thought, wasn't trying to hide this divorce thing at all.

Tessa Mae's mother always commented on how cute Dixie Lee had fixed up her place. Now Tessa Mae could see for herself. There were ruffles everywhere—on the curtains, on lampshades, and on pillows scattered on the couch. One pink satin pillow read "Arkansas State Fair." Crocheted doilies were draped over all the chair arms and head rests and were under ashtrays and candy dishes on the table. It would sure be a lot of trouble to dust here, Tessa Mae thought. On the living room wall there was an embroidered sampler in a frame that read, "Bless This House," and another in the kitchen that read, "Be of Cheerful Heart." In a corner of the kitchen was a what-not shelf with a collection of salt and pepper shakers. Dixie Lee showed Tessa Mae and her mama the ones her husband had brought her from St. Louis on his last trip.

There was a stack of movie magazines in a rack by the

living room couch and Tessa Mae paged through one while her mama and Dixie Lee chattered and fixed lunch. She'd just found an article about two movie stars who were getting a divorce when Dixie Lee came in from the kitchen.

"You want an R.C. Cola or a Grapette, Tessa Mae, honey?" Dixie Lee had on a ruffly apron over her Sunday dress.

Tessa Mae chose an R.C. because it was bigger, and then she ate two tuna fish sandwiches while her mama and Dixie Lee kept talking. They didn't seem to be saying anything worth hearing, but she listened with half her attention just in case.

"When will the divorce be final?" Dixie Lee asked.

"I imagine it'll take some months," Mama answered as she picked at her food.

"I'm going over to the house, Mama." Tessa Mae stood up. "Thank you very much for the lunch, Miz Tooley."

"You're welcome, Tessa Mae." Dixie Lee held a cigarette between scarlet-tipped fingers. "Now don't you go speakin' to any boys on yer way home, you hear? Yer getting to be a real pretty girl. Wish I had hair that long and that pretty color." She laughed and winked at Tessa Mae's mother.

People always commented on Tessa Mae's hair color. It wasn't red or yellow, but some shade in between.

"Land sakes," Mama said. "I was married at sixteen, but I don't think Tessa Mae even has a boyfriend yet, Dixie Lee. All that girl does is read, it seems to me." Her mama and Dixie Lee laughed some more.

Tessa Mae escaped quickly, thinking about the books she'd left at home. Mama wouldn't have packed any of them. She hurried over to the little house and changed out of her Sunday dress. Then she got out her blue jeans and, not finding any scissors, sawed off the legs with her knife. They came out ragged, but Tessa Mae didn't care. They'd be cool. She looked at the bare room again. Yes, if she had to stay here in town, she needed to get her books. Not that she owned many, but she had two checked out from the Lamar Library, and one from the eighth-grade room that she should return.

Hurriedly she left her mother a note. She didn't think she'd care if Tessa Mae went back home to get more things, but it was safer not to wait until she got home to ask her.

Sometimes Aunt Maudie left Uncle Elbert long enough to go to church, but Tessa Mae hadn't seen her that morning. She decided to stop long enough to say hello and make sure they were all right. If her daddy happened to be there for Sunday dinner, so much the better.

"Hey there, Tessa Mae." Aunt Maudie was still in the kitchen, and it smelled like roast and browned potatoes, Tessa Mae's favorite meal next to fried chicken.

"You still in town?" Aunt Maudie was drying dishes, so Tessa Mae pulled out a drawer, got another dish towel, and started to help.

"Me and Mama ate lunch at Dixie Lee Tooley's," Tessa Mae said. Now it was clear that Maudie and Elbert didn't know what was going on with Roy Glen and her mama.

"Where's Uncle Elbert?" Tessa Mae couldn't resist turning over a bowl on the back of the stove and helping herself to a chunk of roast.

"He's takin' a nap. He didn't feel too good this mornin', so I decided I'd better stay home. I don't like leavin' him alone anyway, but there's no one I kin get to come in. You want some more lunch, Tessa Mae? There's plenty."

"No, I jist couldn't resist a bite of yer roast. We had tuna sandwiches."

"Tuna sandwiches for Sunday dinner? That's a shame. Why didn't you and yer mama come over here? Is Roy Glen down in those woods again, too busy to eat?"

"I reckon." No, Maudie didn't know, but it wasn't Tessa

Mae's place to make an announcement that was so serious. Roy Glen would tell Maudie and Elbert in his own good time. And as far as her and her mama coming here for dinner anytime without Roy Glen, it wasn't something they'd made a habit of doing anyway. Since Elbert was Roy Glen's brother, Mama had never been as sociable as she would have with her own blood kin.

"Well, under the circumstances, Tessa Mae, I think you'd better sit down here and have yerself a piece of this cherry pie. I know you've got room."

"We just finished dishes and I'm dirtyin' them again." Tessa Mae protested, but she wasn't going to pass up Aunt Maudie's cherry pie.

"They'll wash, honey, they'll wash. I don't like you bein' so skinny all the time. Lands, if you turned sideways no one would see you."

"You're jist jealous, Aunt Maudie," Tessa Mae teased. She figured her aunt weighed nearly two hundred pounds.

"Maybe so, but I wouldn't know how to act with all those bones showin'. And Elbert says I'm comfortable and warm to sleep by."

Tessa Mae had trouble picturing Elbert and Maudie sleeping together, but then she always had trouble picturing grown-ups in the same bed. Take the Reverend Mr. Peterson and his wife, for example. She couldn't imagine him in a pair of striped pajamas, or worse yet, pajamas with diamond shapes since he was so fond of diamonds. The hardest to imagine was Mama and Roy Glen. At least she didn't have to think about that anymore.

"I declare, Tessa Mae, yer mind wanders off as often as Roy Glen's does. Penny fer yer thoughts." Aunt Maudie had poured herself a cup of coffee and settled down at the kitchen table next to Tessa Mae.

Tessa Mae shook her head. "I guess I've got me some secrets you'd laugh at."

"I believe that, but probably not so different from the secrets I had when I was yer age."

Aunt Maudie was dead wrong about that. Tessa Mae had a different secret that was plaguing her now. She wanted to tell it. She wanted someone to talk to badly, but she kept quiet.

"I reckon if I can walk after eatin' all this pie, I'd better keep goin' on my errand, Aunt Maudie. Tell Uncle Elbert I said hi." She took her plate to the sink and rinsed it off.

"I'll do that." Aunt Maudie smiled at her. "You come back real soon, you hear? With Glennys in Oklahoma City and Ewan off no telling where in that army, I get powerful lonesome sometimes."

"I will, Aunt Maudie," she promised.

Walking home, Tessa Mae thought about Aunt Maudie's kids, grown and gone off to seek their fortunes. She wished she were old enough to go to faraway places where there was some exploring to do. Of course, her daddy was an explorer. He had found an Indian mummy once, as fine as any in Egypt. It was a wondrous thing, but scary if you looked at it at night.

Sometimes the two miles home was long and sometimes short. Today she hadn't worn her shoes, so it seemed long since the sidewalk burned underfoot. Finally the pavement left off and she could walk alongside the dusty road. It was hot for May. Summer in town was going to be a misery. Tessa Mae was tempted to keep on going down to the big swimming hole on the river, but on Sunday afternoon it would be full of kids, and Tessa Mae didn't want to talk to anyone.

She knew that tomorrow Jec would wonder where she

was when she wasn't on the bus. They weren't allowed to sit together, but she always gave him a nod when he got on and he'd grin back. After she and the other white kids got off, the driver would take the colored kids to their school.

Maybe Jec would be glad to have her gone. She wouldn't get him in trouble with Bertha anymore. He'd take up with a bunch of boys and start hanging around wherever it was the colored teenagers favored. The white boys liked the Esso station, which had a garage attached, and Lu's tavern, which had two pinball machines. Tessa Mae always avoided walking past either place.

The house was cool, but it was as empty as when they'd left. Roy Glen must still be off down by the river. Tessa Mae poured herself the last of the iced tea and sat in a rocker on the sleeping porch, wondering what her mother would do if she just picked up and moved back here. Roy Glen could come and go as he pleased. She could take care of herself. Roy Glen wouldn't have to pay any attention to her at all if he didn't want to.

Taking the library books from the small shelf in her bedroom, she decided to leave the rest of her books. After all, she didn't want to get too much of her stuff moved into town. She wasn't going to stay there long.

"No. I'm not goin' to stay in town long," she said aloud. She liked this new idea.

CHAPTER
SEVEN

"I'm sorry about the breakfast, Tessa Mae," Mama said the next morning. "I'll get us some groceries after work today." She had brought the tea kettle from home, and now she spooned out Postum, filling Tessa Mae's cup, and put another box of powdered sugar doughnuts on the table.

"Here's a quarter for school lunch," she said, reaching into her purse and taking out the money. "And the two dollars you wanted. You kin go to Repan's after school and buy what you need. I'm goin' to tell the ladies at work that you'll be babysittin' now, so you kin earn some money real soon. Then you kin have all the clothes you want."

Tessa Mae let her ramble on. Her mother would find out soon enough that she had other plans.

Walking to school felt strange, even though on nice days she had walked the two miles from home. She wouldn't have figured that anyone at school had had time to hear about the divorce, but she was wrong. Somehow the news had leaked out.

Erline Crider didn't usually speak to her unless she had something smart alecky to say, but this morning, all of a sudden, Erline acted friendly. "Morning, Tessa Mae. I hear your mama and daddy are getting a divorce." Erline pronounced it *dee-vorce*. "I never knew of anyone 'cept movie stars doing that. What are you going to do?"

Tessa Mae felt her face grow hot, but she remembered to talk proper, at least. "I don't know, Erline. Maybe I'll just go into the woods and live by myself like Mr. Thoreau."

"Oh, Tessa Mae. You're a scream. You know you can't do that." Erline giggled, then ran over to Sue Anne and the rest of her gang.

After Erline whispered in her ear Sue Anne waved and sashayed over to Tessa Mae. "I hear you're going to become a hermit, Tessa Mae. Think you'll be writing a book about your experiences real soon?"

"Why that's a fine idea, Sue Anne," Tessa Mae answered. "I just guess I'll have to dedicate the book to you, since you were the one who thought of it. Maybe it'll make you famous, too."

Then she walked away, leaving Sue Anne standing there with her mouth hanging open.

Sitting in class, Tessa Mae felt as if everyone was looking at her. She opened her history book and tried hopelessly to concentrate on the presidential election of 1936. It wasn't hard to figure out how people had found out so soon. The preacher must have told his wife. She must have told her friends at church, and they must have told their friends. Tessa Mae had seen Erline Crider's mother whispering with Loralou Peterson in the choir many times.

When class was dismissed for lunch, Miss Criswell, who was Tessa Mae's home room teacher, asked her to stay for a moment. "I heard about your trouble, Tessa Mae. If there's anything I can do, would you let me know?"

Tessa Mae sat silently, her eyes straight ahead.

"Will you be living with your mother?"

Tessa Mae got up from her desk. She was taller than Miss Criswell. "I don't know," she said and headed for the school grounds, desperate to escape but knowing that would give everyone even more to talk about.

"My goodness, Tessa Mae." Sue Anne Sparks sauntered up to her. "Your life has surely got interesting of late."

"I reckon it has," she replied, trying to stay calm. "They'll probably want to make it into a movie pretty soon. I'm trying to decide which movie star should play me. Right now I'm favoring Miz Barbara Stanwyck if she isn't too short."

Sue Anne put her hand over her mouth and giggled. Hurriedly she went to report back to Erline Crider.

Tessa Mae got through the afternoon by pulling a shell around her like an old wood terrapin, ignoring the stares of classmates and the sympathetic, yet curious, glances of several teachers. After school she hurried toward town to implement a plan that had been taking shape all day. The two dollars from her mother and the sixty-nine cents she'd saved would buy food for some time if she was careful.

Walking up and down the aisles of Miller's grocery Tessa Mae compared prices and counted her money several times. Five cans of Campbell's soup were fifty cents; three Baby Ruth candy bars and two of Hershey's chocolate—the ones that were in little squares and could be eaten one piece at a time—twenty-five cents; a bunch of bananas, fifteen cents. She wished she'd checked to see what supplies were still at the house. There would probably be coffee and tea. She bought a quart of milk, a jar of peanut butter, a big box of crackers, and was debating over strawberry preserves or grape jam when she heard a hiss and a whisper from the next aisle.

"Hey there, Tessa Mae." Jec peeked around a display of crackers. "I was hopin' to see you, but pretend like we was two spies and not supposed to know each other." Jec looked all around as if to spot the enemy. "I'm sorry I hollered at you the other day at the swimmin' hole. Mama sure was mad. But I got me a part-time job fer the summer."

Tessa Mae continued to study the jam but whispered loudly. "Where are you working?"

"At the mill. Why wasn't you on the bus?"

"My mama made me move to town, Jec. She's gettin' a divorce from my daddy."

Jec's eyes got big. "Whooooeee, that's somethin'. But you cain't live in town, Tessa Mae. When'll you go fishin'?"

"Well, you've jist happened in on me makin' a well-planned getaway. Like in that movie from Saturday a week ago." Tessa Mae and Jec kept up on the movies pretty well, but they couldn't go together because Jec had to sit in the colored section in the balcony.

"Yeah, I saw that one. You goin' to hide out in an old deserted house?"

"No, I'm going to hide out in my own house."

When a clerk came down the aisle, Tessa Mae pretended she was inspecting the labels on the jelly. "Boy. Hey you, boy." The clerk was yelling at Jec. Tessa Mae moved to the end of the row so she could watch. "Get what you want and get out, you hear? I don't want the likes of you hangin' around my store."

It wasn't his store any more than it was Jec's. The clerk was just showing off by running Jec out.

"Yessir," Jec said to the clerk. "I was just checkin' to see if I had enough money." He pulled some coins from his pocket and slowly counted them out while the clerk went back to the cash register. Tessa Mae knew that Jec always had money, and he always knew how much he carried in his pocket.

As he passed by Tessa Mae with a cup of strawberry ice cream, his favorite, she whispered, "Meet me at my place and I'll tell you my plan."

"Okay, I'll see if I think it'll work."

"I'll see you in about a half hour."

"Not if I see you first."

Tessa Mae grinned, glad to see Jec again. It was like old times.

She practically ran to the rented house, got her blanket, rolled it back up, and then left her mama a note.

> *Dear Mama,*
> *Don't try to find me. I'll be fine. I'm going to*
> *live with Roy Glen. Don't worry about me.*
> *Love,*
> *Tessa Mae*

She signed it *love* even though she wasn't sure she meant it right then. Anyway, the note would stop Mama worrying about where she was or, worse yet, coming after her. Tessa Mae had her own life to live now.

Before she got halfway home, her grocery sack got heavy and the bedroll kept banging her legs. She didn't want to drop and break the peanut butter or the jam. They'd have to last until she could find Roy Glen.

At the house she unloaded her provisions and put the milk in the refrigerator. She'd had a nickel left over for a Dixie cup of chocolate ice cream, her number-one favorite flavor. Luckily, it hadn't melted on the walk home. She was carrying the Dixie cup to the back steps, carefully prying up the lid, when Jec slipped around the side of the four o'clock bushes, looking back, as if something or someone was following him.

"You got a tail?" asked Tessa Mae, remembering all the spy movies they'd seen.

Jec grinned. "Nah, I was jist practicin'. I got June Allyson on my Dixie cup lid. Who'd you git? I got too many June Allysons."

"Carmen Miranda," Tessa Mae announced, licking the melted ice cream that had stuck to the lid, then peeling off the waxed paper to see the photo better. "I'll trade," she offered. "Has Dee-Dee got Carmen Miranda?"

Jec's sister had a big collection of movie star lids. So did Tessa Mae, but she hadn't felt as excited about them the last couple of years.

"Jec . . ." Tessa Mae made another decision while she slipped a bite of chocolate from the wooden spoon and scraped around the edge to level off the ice cream left in the cup. "I'll git out my whole collection of lids fer Dee-Dee. They're under my bed."

"You certain?" Jec asked. "She'd be plumb tickled."

"I don't think I'm goin' to have time fer them. Besides I got to unclutter my life in case I have to pack in a hurry."

"What are you fixin' to do, Tessa Mae? Run away?" Jec looked surprised but Tessa Mae knew he'd favor the plan if she made it up.

"First I'm goin' to move back here, into my real house. Then I'll look for my daddy and see if I kin stay with him where he's diggin'." Roy Glen had surely had time to change his mind by now. With the summer coming on, he would be spending more and more time camping in the woods and hunting relics. Often he let orders pile up until bad weather gave him the time to fill them. If he wouldn't let Tessa Mae camp with him, she'd live in the house by herself. She could even learn to fill the orders when he was too busy. She knew his stock pretty well. They could operate the business together.

"You're runnin' away from yer mama? What'll she say about that?" Jec asked. "Bet she won't like it. Bet she won't let you do it."

Jec had been around Tessa Mae's mama enough to know her ways, but this time he just had to be wrong. She crossed fingers on both hands to take the hex off the thought.

"I don't think she kin stop me, Jec. I left her a note so she wouldn't worry. I'm glad you found me in the store. I was afraid you wasn't ever goin' to speak to me again."

"My mama said us bein' seen together, big as you are, could git us in trouble. Especially me."

"She told me I could git you killed, Jec. I think she was jist mad at us, but I sure wouldn't want to git you killed. You think that could happen?"

"Not if I had a chance to run. I kin run fast."

"I don't want to git you into trouble, Jec. You know that. But I figure I need my only friend right now. You're the only one I kin count on."

"I'm glad to be of help when my friend, Miz Barbara Stanwyck, is going to have an adventure."

Barbara Stanwyck was definitely Tessa Mae's favorite movie star, and her roles always called for her to be in trouble. Either her husband was trying to poison her or someone else was trying to scare her to pieces. Lately, Tessa Mae was feeling more and more like Miz Stanwyck. No one was trying to kill her, of course, but just thinking about the changes that had been taking place in her life could get her pretty scared.

Sitting on the back steps, it felt like any other day before the bad things happened so they fell right into playing the movie star initial game.

"V.L." Tessa Mae called out to get them started.

"Easy. That's Miz Veronica Lake with her hair in her eyes so she cain't hardly see where she's goin' and some handsome guy has to take her hand."

Tessa Mae laughed. She liked being with Jec better than anyone in the whole world.

"H.B.," he challenged.

"Humphrey Bogart. Remember how he had that hideout from all them Germans? You and me kin have a hideout. You kin bring me some of your mama's corn bread so I won't starve."

"This is goin' to be fun, Tessa Mae. I'll bet your mama skins you alive, though. You jist wait and see if she don't."

"Well, I'm not going to worry about it," she said firmly. "E.W."

"Anybody'd know that's yer next-favorite star, Esther Williams, the swimming sensation." Jec was teasing, but Tessa Mae was proud that she had even mastered some of those underwater swimming tricks herself.

Thinking about swimming, even by herself, being friends with Jec, even in secret, and living in her house, even if alone, Tessa Mae felt the emptiness and the fear that had been building up inside her begin to melt away.

CHAPTER
EIGHT

There were signs that Roy Glen had been to the office, but it was hard to tell how long he'd stayed. He'd probably checked the piles of mail on his desk, got some supplies, then taken off again. There was a dirty coffee cup in the kitchen sink and some cold grounds in the pot. Out of habit Tessa Mae rinsed it out and turned it upside down on the dryer rack.

She hid the rest of her groceries under her bed along with her shoes and bedroll, so Mama wouldn't find them if she came looking for her. The dust was so thick, she sneezed twice before she reached the cigar box with her collection of movie star lids.

"Do you think we can go to yer place, Jec?" She wiped off the cigar box and put it under her arm.

"I reckon. Mama never told me not to invite you home."

"I guess if she don't want me there, I kin leave." Staying in her house by herself was beginning to feel real lonely. It was so silly. She was the one who thought she could go off in the woods like Thoreau. But maybe Thoreau had more time to get used to the idea.

She pulled the back door shut, not bothering to lock it. Nobody in Lamar locked a house, except maybe the people who owned the big houses over on the highway. Mostly, there was nothing in Lamar anyone would want to steal.

"I'm starving, Jec. Reckon your mama will let me stay to dinner?" The thought of Bertha's corn bread and turnip greens was making her stomach rumble.

"I s'pose so, Tessa Mae. Let's run. I'm real hungry too."

The closer they got to Jec's house, the more uneasy he seemed. "Tell you what, Tessa Mae. You sit here on this stump and I'll go in and tell Mama you jist dropped by to visit. That might be better than surprisin' her."

As Tessa Mae waited for Jec, the fear came flooding back. Now she figured that Bertha *had* told Jec he wasn't to see Tessa Mae at all.

Jec returned, grinning. "Mama said as long as you're already here, you might as well come in. I told her you stopped by with a present for Dee-Dee."

Tessa Mae knew Jec hadn't told his mama that they'd walked over here together.

"Howdy, Tessa Mae." Bertha's face was beaded with sweat as she poured corn bread batter into a cast-iron skillet greased with bacon drippings so hot it was smoking. It sizzled and snapped until Bertha popped it into the oven. "Ain't it kinda late fer you to be down here? Your mama'll be needin' you to start dinner."

"Her mama's done run away to town to get a divorce," Jec announced.

Tessa Mae hadn't been sure what she was going to tell Bertha. Now she told her everything. Bertha kept turning chicken and stirring green beans. Then she mashed up a big pot of potatoes, dumping in a cube of butter and a cup of milk.

"So I guess Mama forgot that she won't be needin' you on Saturday," Tessa Mae said. The fried chicken smelled so good she could hardly concentrate on what she was saying.

"Well, ain't that a lick?" Bertha said. "I never heard tell of such a thing. But where you supposed to be, Tessa Mae?"

"I'm supposed to be in town with my mama. But I didn't like it there, so I'm back at the house. I guess I'll go lookin' fer my daddy tomorrow."

"Yer stayin' at that house by yourself? You cain't do that, girl. Yer mama will worry."

"I left her a note. I don't think she'll much care what I do."

"What a misery." Bertha shook her head and reached in the oven to flip over the corn bread. The top was crispy and brown. Tessa Mae knew the middle would be moist and golden.

"Kin she eat supper with us?" Jec was setting plates on the big table. The patterns were all the same, even though some were cracked or stained. Rose Ann followed Jec with the silverware, placing it carefully beside the plates.

"I reckon so." Bertha seemed resigned to Tessa Mae being there. "Go get your daddy, Jec. And tell the kids to wash up. Tessa Mae, you kin pour the buttermilk."

Tessa Mae got the heavy crockery pitcher from the ice box, glad Bertha had given her a job. She didn't want to be a guest. In fact, she wished she was part of this big family.

There were nine Browns at the table. Everet, the oldest, was sixteen and worked at the mill east of town. Florella, fourteen, had a figure that was rounded a lot more than Tessa Mae's. It didn't seem to bother Florella, though, flouncing around the kitchen in a calico dress.

Rose Ann, nine, was the most help to her mother. She looked after the little ones and helped Bertha with the cooking and the washing. Dee-Dee was Jec's pet and everyone's favorite. Tessa Mae knew that she wasn't ever going to be very smart, but she had a sweet smile and caused no trouble for anyone.

"What did you bring me, Tessa Mae?" Dee-Dee asked. "Jec brought me two new lids—'cept I already had June Allyson. Who was that other one, Jec?"

"Carmen Miranda," he told her. "You know, the lady who dances with a basket of fruit on her head."

"Like this, Dee-Dee." Florella jumped up, held a bowl of turnip greens on her head, and started wiggling her hips.

"You sit down there and eat, Florella. Pass your daddy some more mashed potatoes." Bertha ruled her family with an iron hand, but most of the kids, especially Jec, managed to slip out from under it pretty often. There were times when Bertha's word was law, though, like that evening at the swimming hole.

Rose Ann cut up part of her chicken breast for Lilly Belle and handed baby Harry, in his high chair, a drumstick to gnaw on. Lilly Belle was six and always smiling. Tiny braids stuck up all over her head where Rose Ann had plaited her hair.

Mr. Joses Brown was a tall, thin quiet man, half the size of Bertha if you measured around instead of up and down. He didn't bother with telling the children what to do, at least not when Tessa Mae was around. He left all the disciplining of the kids up to Bertha. Or, maybe he just didn't feel natural around white folks, even Tessa Mae. Everet, as quiet as his daddy, ignored her, too.

No one took much time to talk as the evening meal quickly disappeared. Tessa Mae bit into her hot corn bread, glazed with butter, knowing her diet of peanut butter and crackers would get old fast. "This is awful good corn bread, Bertha," she said. "My mama never learned to make it this good."

"Your mama's biscuits beats mine, though, Tessa Mae. What's your daddy goin' to do, tryin' to manage on his own? Bet he cain't cook nothin' but coffee."

"He does pretty good on a campfire, Bertha. Guess he'll eat beans and Spam mostly. He don't seem to pay much attention to food anyway."

"You tell him to stop by here every once in a while for some home-cooked meals, you hear?" Bertha offered, starting the platter of chicken around again. Bertha liked to feed people. The Browns might be poor by some standards, but they ate well. The big garden out back provided them a good harvest. Bertha canned what they couldn't eat. She worked at the peach shed in season in trade for peaches, and Everet worked with his father at the mill now.

"Now you be sure to tell him," Bertha repeated.

"I sure will." If I can find him, Tessa Mae thought. She sipped her cold buttermilk and then took a second helping of everything.

"I'll help with the cleanin' up, Bertha," Tessa Mae offered when people finally pushed away from the table.

"Florella and Rose Ann kin do it, Tessa Mae. But I'd be obliged if you and Jec would look after the little ones for a spell."

"Aw, Mama, I had plans," Florella grumbled.

"You ain't got no plans tonight, Florella, 'cept doin' dishes and changin' baby Harry's diaper. And don't you go thinkin' otherwise."

Florella had thought otherwise. Her shoulders slumped and she picked up the baby reluctantly. "Come on, you old baby. You a mess."

Tessa Mae and Jec took Dee-Dee and Lilly Belle out on the front steps. Mr. Joses Brown leaned his chair against the porch wall and lit a pipe of sweet-smelling tobacco. The smoke's aroma mingled with the scent of hydrangeas that Bertha had planted near the door. Everet had disappeared.

Dee-Dee squealed when Tessa Mae gave her the box of movie star pictures. She got her own full shoe box and started matching up the pairs and triples.

Crickets started their nightly concert, and a mockingbird began to sing. The first star appeared in the fading light, and Tessa Mae made her wish: to be a part of a happy family, not one that was breaking up like a rowboat in a storm on the river.

The sound of Bertha, Rose Ann, and Florella clattering dishes together in the kitchen drifted out of the small frame house. Then Bertha started singing a snatch or two of "Have I Done My Best for Jesus?" Florella joined in with a sweet soprano voice, and Rose Ann sang harmony.

Dee-Dee had three rows of movie stars lined up, and Jec leaned over to prove to her that Ronald Coleman and Gary Cooper were two different people. Lilly Belle giggled as she ran after a hop toad headed for the garden.

"I got to go home now, Jec, 'fore it gets too dark. Tell yer mama I said thanks fer the good dinner." Tessa Mae brushed aside a tear before Jec could see it.

"Ain't you scared to stay in that big old house by yerself, Tessa Mae?" Jec asked. "I would be."

"I ain't scared of anythin', Jec." Tessa Mae jumped up from the step and hit the path running. The soft thud of her bare feet was lost in a chorus of cicadas.

CHAPTER
NINE

The house *was* awfully quiet, but Tessa Mae was so tired that she fell asleep before she could worry about being there alone.

The cardinal woke her, but she lay there for a long time, thinking. She'd probably get in trouble faster for not going to school than she would for running off from her mother. She hadn't missed a day the whole year, except the afternoon she'd played hookey. Now she wished she'd made a habit of being absent occasionally.

There were things that Tessa Mae liked about school. The work was easy for her, and Miss Criswell had given her extra books to read this year from her own home library. And in January she'd asked Tessa Mae to help her choose some new library books. When they came she let Tessa Mae read them first. The one Tessa Mae liked best was the story of Mr. Charles Darwin and how he traveled all over the world discovering new plants and animals.

The longest trip she had ever taken had been to Little Rock with Roy Glen. On the way back they'd stopped in the woods on the Fourche River to see an old man who was selling a papoose carrier, a pair of moccasins, and a tobacco pouch, all over a hundred years old.

When Tessa Mae had seen the carrier, she imagined a squawling baby strapped to the wooden back, unaware of the beauty of the beaded skin that held her tight. There had been hundreds of beads in the design, mostly white, while the colored beads made the pattern. Tessa Mae had begged her daddy not to sell it, but he'd said it was worth a lot of money. He had given her the moccasins and tobacco pouch, though.

She hopped out of the bed on the sleeping porch and searched under the bed in her room for the red shoe box, then took it back to the porch and slipped on the moccasins. They'd been too large when she got them but now they fit just right.

She ran her fingers over the soft buckskin of the moccasins. Their beaded design seemed more elegant than the highest-priced item in the Sears and Roebuck catalogue. The moccasins, the pouch, and the carrier had been handmade with long hours of loving attention. An Indian woman had chewed the skin to make the soft, suede leather. She had carefully sewed on each bead to make the pretty design. The shoes showed no wear. And since the pouch didn't smell of tobacco, it must never have been used either. She often wondered what had happened to keep them so new.

As Tessa Mae fingered the soft skin and shiny beads, she felt a rush of emotion for a woman, a mother, who loved her family so much. She longed for a mother who would sew her a new dress instead of working at the laundry. One who could love her husband and stay with him, working out their problems. One who never stopped loving her baby even when she was no longer a cute, roly-poly child, but a big gawky girl who was "developing."

Tessa Mae figured it was easy to love a cuddly baby who wasn't old enough to have taken on any ways that its mother didn't understand. Mama just didn't understand her, and she didn't understand Roy Glen either. Most likely the time would come when her mama would want to divorce Tessa Mae right along with him.

She wrapped the shoes and pouch back up in tissue paper and placed them carefully in the box. They were worth a lot of money. Her mama had said, "Roy Glen, if that papoose carrier is worth so much, the shoes and pouch are worth a lot, too. Why are you giving them to Tessa Mae instead of selling them? You know we need the money."

"Tessa Mae likes them, Vinnie," her daddy had answered. "The money don't matter none."

Since her mama had grumbled about them, Tessa Mae had always kept the shoes and pouch hidden. Now she put them back under the bed alongside the stamp collection she'd culled from Roy Glen's mail and shoe boxes of paper dolls that she'd almost outgrown.

Over a bowl of corn flakes, Tessa Mae planned her day. She'd do some reading and then late in the afternoon she'd go fishing. Then she'd make herself a good fish dinner. If after a couple or three days, Roy Glen didn't come by, she'd go looking for him.

Today's midday heat was different from summer heat, lighter weight, less oppressive, and welcome. The long summer days she loved had just about arrived. Tessa Mae curled up in the grape arbor, reading until she fell asleep, and dozed for an hour or more.

When the shadows got longer, she headed for Jec's, fishing pole in hand, hoping he was home from school. Maybe they could talk Bertha into going with them, since Tessa Mae knew Jec wouldn't dare go off alone with her again. It was usually an easy job to get Bertha to go fishing.

Jec was sitting on the front porch, whittling a reed whistle for Dee-Dee. He didn't seem surprised to see Tessa Mae, but he pursed his lips and whistled when he heard she'd stayed home all day. "You played hookey?" he asked. "Betcha git in trouble, betcha do."

"I hope not, since I got all the trouble I kin handle. Go ask yer mother if she'll go fishin' with us, Jec."

When Bertha came out of the garden, Jec jumped up and said, "Mama, Tessa Mae and me want to go fishin'. Couldn't we use a mess of fish for supper? Wouldn't you like to sneak off with us and see if you kin catch that old catfish that keeps teasin' you?"

"Wait till I get my pole," Bertha said, not even stopping to think about it. "A mess of catfish is jist what we needs tonight. Whoooeee, I kin taste 'um now."

Bertha was in a good mood and she didn't say a word about it not being right for Tessa Mae to be along. She loved to fish, and she was good at it, keeping her family's diet supplemented with catfish and bass. Dee-Dee and Lilly Belle ran after them, but Bertha stopped them and called, "Florella, you watch after these young'uns, you hear? And tell Rose Ann to peel some potatoes and wash me a mess of greens. I'm gonna come home with a big string of catfish for supper."

"Aw, Mama, why cain't I go fishin' too?" Florella complained. "I been workin' hard all day."

Bertha had kept Florella home from school to help with the wash and the strawberry preserves. "'Cause I need you here at home, Missy. I been workin' all day too."

"Abe Pokewith asked Florella to marry up with him," Jec confided as they followed behind Bertha's bulk down the trail to the river. "Mama said she'd think on it. I sure feel sorry for Florella quittin' school and havin' to tend to a little baby."

Abe Pokewith worked at the mill with Everet. Tessa Mae had seen him once with Everet in town on a Saturday. "I reckon that's what Florella wants to do, Jec," Tessa Mae said.

"I cain't even think on gettin' married, kin you, Tessa Mae?"

"No, but you and I ain't eighteen like Abe Pokewith. I reckon you'll change your mind, Jec." Tessa Mae grinned. She caught up with Bertha. "You goin' to let Florella get married?" With Bertha so relaxed, it was easy for Tessa Mae to forget that Bertha had ever been mad at her.

"I'm thinkin' on it," Bertha answered. "With that gal so hot after him and already in trouble, it might be the best thing to do. She's goin' to be through with eighth grade this year. I guess that's plenty of schoolin' for raisin' babies. Florella's so smart, I figured she might be my first child to go to high school. Now it'll have to be Jec or Rose Ann."

Tessa Mae was going to be finished with eighth grade too, but she couldn't imagine herself getting married. Bertha seemed to read her mind. "Some folks mature faster than others, girl. Don't you go thinkin' on gettin' married, Tessa Mae. You got to go on to high school too."

"Don't worry, Bertha. I don't think I'm ready to git married. I might never git married. I'm goin' to travel and explore places. Maybe even way far off places like Africa."

"Ummm-ummm. Such ideas you got, Tessa Mae. I reckon I got me some kinfolks over there in Africa. You tell 'em I said hi, you hear?"

"I might go along to Africa, too, Mama," Jec said. "I'll tell 'em hi."

There was a bed of spearmint to wade through before they reached the river, and the fragrance of the bruised leaves enveloped them. They picked out comfortable places to sit on the bank of the river where leafy trees formed a canopy of shade. The river ran deep and had dug out a section of the bank so it edged a pool that catfish favored.

Tessa Mae settled in, let her line drop in the pool and waited. All thoughts dropped away for a time while she dozed. Then a flop and a splash of water signaled that Bertha had hooked a fish. She yanked it up onto the bank. It was a big one. Hanging it onto a forked stick by running the stick through a gill, Bertha baited her hook and tossed it back in.

Checking her hook to make sure she still had her bait, Tessa Mae realized she'd never been fishing with Bertha when Bertha didn't catch fish. In fact, she had hooked several by the time Tessa Mae felt the tug on her line. Jerking upward, she pulled her line back from the deep pool. The fish was gone. She had yanked too soon and lost it. The same thing happened two more times before Bertha came over and sat beside her.

She had on a floppy old straw hat and a faded blue dress. Tessa Mae could smell the sweat that beaded her upper lip and turned her brown arms shiny. Not an unpleasant odor, it was comforting, reminding Tessa Mae of the times she'd watched Bertha iron. Since Mama had gone to work, Bertha was the one she always talked to, and ironing was a special time to visit.

"What's the matter, girl? Yer coming up empty too often."

To her dismay, Tessa Mae started to cry. "Seems like my whole life is comin' up empty lately, Bertha."

Bertha's arms went around her, and Tessa Mae leaned her head on Bertha's soft, ample breasts.

"I know, child. Yer having your share of misery now."

"I don't know what to do, Bertha. I wish things was back like they always was. Mama goin' to work was bad enough, but now it seems all she wants in her life is things. A prettier house with ruffles and pillows on the couch. Pretty clothes and dishes. And no people."

"Your mama wants you in her life, Tessa Mae. What's happenin' to yer mama and yer daddy has got nothin' to do with you. They're havin' their troubles, and they may think they cain't get along together no more, but they both still love you, child. You got to understand that."

"I cain't, Bertha. It don't make no sense to me. I don't want to live in town with Mama, and it appears my daddy don't want me to live out here in the woods with him. I don't know what to do."

"The Lord will give you a sign, Tessa Mae. If you'll let Him, He'll help you through this and He'll help you decide what to do."

Tessa Mae had looked for the signs Bertha kept talking about. But something else was on her mind, something that was giving Tessa Mae almost as much pain as her mama and daddy breaking up. Tessa Mae gathered the courage to bring it up.

"Bertha, there's something else."

"What is it, baby?"

"I—I—cain't give up bein' friends with you and Jec and Rose Ann and Dee-Dee. With my mama in town and Roy Glen sayin' he don't want me, I cain't stop comin' over to see you, too. I just cain't."

"I reckon you got a point there, Tessa Mae. I'll tell you what. Let's make us a rule and stick by it. You and Jec kin keep bein' friends and of course, you and me, but only down here with all the family together. You come to our house anytime you like. How about that?"

Tessa Mae hugged Bertha and her eyes got blurry again as she nodded agreement. She blinked several times to clear them up. Anything was better than giving up Jec altogether.

"But I declare, child, I thought we'd taught you to be a better fisherman than to ignore that old catfish nibblin' on your line."

Sure enough, Tessa Mae's pole was bending over slightly at the end. Not so anxious this time, she tugged firmly at the line and the weight felt secure. Out onto the bank, she flopped a catfish bigger than any she'd ever caught.

"I do believe you've caught that old fish I've been lookin' for all year, Tessa Mae." Bertha unhooked the fish for Tessa Mae, careful of the barbs on either side of his head.

"Yer luck brought him over here, Bertha," Tessa Mae said. "Take him home."

"What say we share him? If you and Jec will clean these, we'll have us a big fish fry tonight. I'll wilt down some greens with bacon drippin's and make us some hush puppies. And I made three strawberry-rhubarb pies this mornin'. Come on, girl, my mouth is startin' to water."

Tessa Mae looked at the large string of fish.

They'd be a lot of work to clean, but more than worth it. All members of a big family did their share of the work, and they had their share of the fun—or the eating, as would be the case tonight. She'd be pleased to do her share, to follow any rule that allowed her to share Bertha's family. She needed desperately to be a part of something, on any terms.

CHAPTER
TEN

What day was it? she wondered. Wednesday? Tessa Mae, eating her cereal in the late morning sun, counted she'd been alone only a day and two nights, but already it was starting to feel comfortable. Of course, eating dinner at the Browns' both nights was cheating. And now she was going to cheat again because Bertha had invited her to church with them tonight.

Tessa Mae loved to go to Wednesday night prayer meetings at the colored church. She was even willing to believe that if Bertha was right and the Lord was fixing to give her a sign, it would be there. *Be patient all ye that love the Lord*, the Bible said. But how much longer was she expected to wait?

She washed her few dishes and had settled in the grape arbor to study, when she heard a car turn into the driveway.

Peeking out of the arbor, she saw it was Dixie Lee Tooley's truck. Dixie Lee and her mama both got out and went into the house.

Tessa Mae tried to remember. All the dishes were put away. Her bed was made, so maybe it wouldn't be obvious that she'd slept there last night. With luck her mother would think that she was staying with Roy Glen.

The two women were going in and out, letting the back door slam every trip. They were probably carrying dishes, curtains, and rugs. She knew it was risky to keep crawling forward to look out; she sat so still that Mr. Inky slid over her toes, looking for a better spot to nap. His skin felt slick and cool, and Tessa Mae marveled at the way he slid forward with so little effort and no sound. When he came close she always wanted to reach out and pet him, but it didn't seem right somehow. He always appeared to listen when she spoke to him, but he kept his distance and she never touched him.

Her mother and Dixie Lee were laughing while they piled things into the truck. From the sound of it Mama certainly wasn't grieving. Tessa Mae crawled closer to the opening of the arbor, wondering if they'd leave anything for her and Roy Glen. If her mother looked under her bed and spotted the bedroll, she'd know for sure that Tessa Mae was there.

The door slammed again and then there was a more metallic slam, as they put up the truck's gate and chained it shut.

"Tessa Mae. Are you in there? Answer me, you hear?" Her mother's voice reached her in the shady arbor. Tessa Mae sat still, hardly breathing.

Her mother waited. "Tessa Mae, I want you to come into town with me," she finally called. "You cain't stay here alone. I don't want you to stay here alone."

"Is she in there, Vinnie?" Dixie Lee asked.

"I don't know," her mother answered. "She may be off down in the woods somewhere. I stopped tryin' to keep track of where she got off to. I guess that was wrong of me, but I never worried about it until recently. She's growed up of late and is gettin' so pretty. She's got to get settled down. It ain't safe or decent for her to be runnin' wild down here in these woods."

Tessa Mae waited, listening. She waited where she was for a long time, until she heard the truck doors slam and the rumble of the engine.

A robin's song resuming in the chinaberry tree signaled that the intruders had gone. That and the fact that she was hungry propelled her out of the arbor. She knew her mama had to get back to work.

There was a note on the kitchen table.

Dear Tessa Mae,
Your daddy was in town and he said you
wasn't with him. I'm worried about you. So is
he. I want you to come home. I need you with
me. I love you.

Mama

Home. Where was home these days? A tear rolled down Tessa Mae's cheek and dropped on the tablet paper. Mama didn't really need her. She had her job and a place in town to fix up. Despite what she'd said, Tessa Mae knew she'd only get in her way. Her mama hadn't said she loved her in a long time, but even so, the note sounded like another of Mama's plans to get her own way.

Feeling confused and empty, Tessa Mae smeared a stack of crackers with peanut butter and put them in a paper bag. Then she filled a mayonnaise jar with ice and poured tea into it. There wasn't any lemon, but she stirred in lots of sugar.

Tessa Mae walked around the silent house, sipping the tea. Her mama had taken some dishes, but left a few, also one fork, knife, and spoon each for her and Roy Glen. Two rockers were gone. Without looking further, she slipped out the back door and walked towards the Browns', then stopped in a small clearing on the river to eat her lunch.

The muddy swirl of greenish-brown water soothed her fear and bolstered her determination to live alone. In the solitude of the woods, her troubles always slipped away into the current, racing down towards wherever the river hurried.

Now that her confidence had returned, it was time to move on. If Mama had seen Roy Glen in town just this morning, he must have bought supplies, then headed back to the house to wash up and check on his orders. She jumped up, threw the jar in the sack, and raced home.

There was no sign of Roy Glen. His shed smelled of stale cigarette smoke and dusty rocks, but the kitchen was just as she'd left it. Still, she waited for him until after supper, reading and doing some math problems. Math was easy now that Jec had helped her get past fractions. In fact, it was a lot less complicated than her life. She chewed the end of her pencil. Nobody seemed to care where she was. Her daddy didn't seem to be looking very hard, and her mother must have just given up. Taking a deep breath, she resolved, Myself. I'll take care of myself.

Determined not to rely on the Browns for dinner again, Tessa Mae ate a peanut butter sandwich and a banana. Then she pulled on a snug print dress. The thin cloth stretched tight across her breasts and armpits, but she couldn't very well wear cut-off jeans and a T-shirt to church.

Carrying her shoes and socks to put on later, Tessa Mae took off down the trail. Being in the woods, her woods, made up for the feeling that she didn't have a home anymore. This was her home, the comforting trees and bushes and the familiar landmarks.

"Hey, Jec, come on out here," she called, then sat on the steps of the Browns' house to put on her shoes.

Jec came out, grinning, and sat beside her, putting on his own pair of brown oxfords with the toes cut out. Bertha bought shoes for her family each fall, and by spring most had thin soles and toes cut out for room.

The colored church was within walking distance down a dirt road. Jec and Tessa Mae led the way, with the rest of the Brown family forming a line behind them. Dee-Dee hurried to join them and they swung her between them. "You in our family now, Tessa Mae?" Dee-Dee asked, smiling up at her.

"Almost, Dee-Dee, almost," Tessa Mae answered, smiling back.

Newly painted and in good repair, the church was a great contrast to the tar-paper shacks that surrounded it. Like the shacks, it crouched on an open foundation of stacked bricks to allow flood waters to flow underneath. A few small trees struggled to survive in the dusty yard, and right up near the doors, someone had planted japonica bushes, forsythia, and lilacs.

The minister of the church, Reverend Gabriel Showalter, worked as a supervisor at the turpentine mill over in Piny Groves. He had a car and could drive to his job, while most of his congregation had to walk. Tonight he wore a black robe over his clothing, but Tessa Mae had seen him plenty of times in a fine dark suit, crisp white shirt, and a red tie. She felt as comfortable here as she did at her church in town—maybe more so. She even liked the sermons, which could stretch on and on for over an hour.

But what Tessa Mae liked best was the singing, especially on prayer meeting nights when the Reverend Showalter started up the service with some hymns. Bertha and Florella sang in the choir. Once the family reached the church, they left Jec and Tessa Mae in charge of the little ones and went to put on their blue robes with big white collars. Jec quickly led his charges to seats on the second row. Dee-Dee settled between Jec and Tessa Mae, and Rose Ann and Lilly Belle sat beside them. Everet and Mr. Brown sat closer to the back, and Tessa Mae noticed that Abe Poke-with sat beside Everet, almost like he was already part of the Browns' family.

The Reverend Showalter rose to stand before the congregation. He waited a moment to heighten the suspense, and then he called for the first hymn. Immediately Tessa Mae and Jec paged through the old shape-note hymnals, looking for their favorites. The hymnals were left over from the days when people learned the tunes from the way the notes were shaped: round, triangle or square.

"Brighten the Corner Where You Are," Jec shouted out. When they'd finished that hymn, Tessa Mae yelled, "Standin' on the Promises."

The widow Stanky called out "When They Ring Them Golden Bells." She sat alone on the front row, a tiny woman with snow-white hair who looked about a hundred years old. Jec and Tessa Mae looked at each other and smiled. They figured she could hear the golden bells already, ringing for her in that land across the river.

By the time the congregation had sung "Rescue the Perishing" and "Bringing in the Sheaves," they were warmed up pretty good. The preacher broke into a long prayer. His deep, mellow voice rang out over the whole church, and everytime he paused for breath or inspiration someone in the congregation would shout, "Amen," or "Praise the Lord."

After the choir gave folks a rest by singing "Softly and Tenderly," they sat down and people began shuffling around to get comfortable, since it was time for the sermon. Reverend Showalter started to preach about how the wicked would be damned for all time and the folks who were good to each other and loved the Lord would get their just reward in heaven. The longer he preached, the more excited his voice sounded, and the congregation encouraged him by shouting, "You tell 'em, Preacher," or "Amen," or "That's the truth."

One time Tessa Mae had got so caught up in the emotion that she called out "Amen." Jec punched her and giggled, but no one else seemed to take any special notice.

Tessa Mae never dozed or daydreamed the way she did at her own church, but after a time, she and Jec helped to entertain Lilly Belle and Dee-Dee by making string figures with a piece of twine Jec carried in his pocket. She could always depend on Jec to be carrying something interesting.

The service ended with three verses of "Wonderful Words of Life" and "Safe in the Arms of Jesus" to give the people something to hold on to until they could get charged up again on Sunday:

> *Safe in the arms of Jesus,*
> *Safe on His gentle breast.*
> *There by His love overshaded,*
> *Sweetly my soul shall rest.*

Tessa Mae always went home from the colored church feeling light-hearted and relieved of her burdens. It had worked again tonight even with her burdens heavier than usual. Leaving the Browns with a good night and a promise to visit again soon, she bounced down the trail singing:

> *Bringing in the sheaves,*
> *Bringing in the sheaves.*
> *We shall come rejoicing,*
> *Bringing in the sheaves.*

As she watched a full moon peek over a hickory nut tree, Tessa Mae felt like rejoicing. The heaviness that had settled in her heart seemed to float away on the warm night air. Maybe God *had* given her a sign, after all. She went to bed intending to get a fresh start on her life first thing in the morning.

CHAPTER
ELEVEN

By morning the good feeling from the prayer meeting had dropped away, and Tessa Mae began to get uneasy about missing school.

She spent the day worrying about falling behind in her assignments and wondering what Miss Criswell thought about her absence. By four o'clock, she knew.

When Sharon Criswell first came to Lamar, there was talk about her being too fancy to be a schoolteacher. She had a little blue Ford, her hair was cut into a pageboy like June Allyson's, and she was so young. How, folks wondered, could a teacher who was still a girl herself control kids in the eighth grade.

Maybe that was why Tessa Mae liked her better than any teacher she'd ever had. Miss Criswell was different, and she didn't have any friends in Lamar, either. People speculated on what she did on Saturday when she took off for Clarksville, the nearest big town. But she was always in church on Sunday morning, sitting alone and smiling all the time. Tessa Mae thought that was probably what bothered people most. They didn't like not knowing what made Miss Criswell so happy.

Tessa Mae was sitting on the back steps when the blue car turned into her driveway and pulled up behind the old Dodge. There was no time to hide, and Tessa Mae wasn't even sure she wanted to.

"Hey, Tessa Mae. There you are. Have you been sick? I've missed you." Miss Criswell had on a pretty plaid dress and stylish wedgie high heels.

Tessa Mae was surprised at how happy she was to see the young teacher.

"I—I didn't like livin' "—she stopped to correct her speech—"living in town. I came back out here."

"That's no reason for not coming to school. You came to school from out here before, didn't you?" Miss Criswell was standing at the bottom of the steps, smiling.

"Yes," Tessa Mae answered. Then, not knowing what to say next, she asked, "Would you like some iced tea?"

"I surely would. I came straight from school and I'm tired." Miss Criswell followed Tessa Mae to the kitchen and sat on one of the straight chairs, looking perfectly at home.

Mama had taken the pretty glasses, but Tessa Mae found a big jelly glass in the back of the cabinet, rinsed it out in case it was dusty, and filled it with ice and tea. She filled the mayonaise jar for herself. "I'm sorry I don't have any lemon," she said, putting a bowl of sugar and a spoon on the table.

"That's all right. I like it plain."

"Mama took the rocking chairs with her to town." Tessa

Mae led the way back to the sleeping porch, feeling she had to explain why the house looked so vacant.

"Let's sit outside in those lawn chairs. I love being outside this time of year. I'll be glad when school is out, won't you? It's hard to stay inside on these nice days." Tessa Mae followed Miss Criswell down the steps to the backyard and they sat under the giant oak tree.

Tessa Mae had never considered the possibility that teachers were glad when school was out. The idea made her want to laugh.

Miss Criswell sipped her tea, then said, "Your yard is lovely, Tessa Mae, and the woods are so close by. I can see why you missed it. If I lived here I'd sit outside and grade papers. But I want you to come back to school. There's not much left and you need your credits to go on to ninth grade next year."

"I might not go on to ninth grade."

"I don't believe that, Tessa Mae. You're too smart. What would you do if you didn't finish school? Work in the laundry?"

"I reckon I could." Tessa Mae studied the amber tea as it swirled over the chunks of ice. She hadn't meant to say "reckon."

Miss Criswell set her tea down on the grass. "Tessa Mae, look at me and be honest. If you could do anything you wanted to right now, or even four years from now, what would it be?"

Tessa Mae didn't hesitate long. She looked up at Miss Criswell and told her, "I'd stay down on the river bottoms with my daddy and dig for Indian relics."

"What kind of things does he find?"

"See that grinding stone, there by the tree?" Tessa Mae pointed to a big rock at the base of the oak tree with a smaller rock sitting in the saucer-like depression. "Indians ground corn in that once. Mostly Roy Glen finds arrowheads, though, and sometimes spearheads, or bone scrapers. Once I found part of a pot, enough to see the design. It was in a farmer's field. We figured it was from a grave, but we couldn't find it. Good relics get harder and harder to find."

Miss Criswell walked over to examine the grinding stones and Tessa Mae followed, proud of herself for using the correct grammar.

"How does your father know where to dig?" Miss Criswell asked.

Tessa Mae shrugged. "Farmers turn up things when they're plowing. They usually don't want them. Sometimes Roy Glen—that's my daddy—pays them a little for digging on their land. Pieces of pottery or beads could mean a grave was there. So he'll dig around and sift out the dirt before the farmer starts planting. It's really exciting to find a grave, and usually Roy Glen knows what Indian tribe was living there by what's in it."

Tessa Mae finally paused for breath, then ran into the house and brought out the shoe box with the beaded moccasins and the tobacco pouch.

"An Indian woman spent a long time making these." She handed the moccasins and pouch to Miss Criswell. "Course, my daddy didn't dig them out of the ground. They would have been rotted away. He traded for them. Feel how soft. Aren't they pretty?"

Miss Criswell fingered the soft buckskin, then slipped off her shoe, and put on the moccasin, laughing. "Too big for me. She probably made them for her husband along with the pouch. She loved him a lot to work so hard, didn't she?"

It hadn't occurred to Tessa Mae that the shoes might be for a man. They fit her. But come to think of it, the Indian

woman was probably as small as or smaller than Miss Criswell. People used to be smaller, and Tessa Mae was already
bigger than most grown men she knew. She was probably
the size of an Indian man long ago.

"Would you like to see some more things in my daddy's
office?"

"Yes, I would, but let's wait a few minutes." Miss Criswell returned to her chair. "Tessa Mae, what would you
think of going to college to study archaeology? That's the
science of studying relics left by ancient peoples, like the
Indians here in Arkansas. You could dig all you wanted to
and get paid for it."

"My daddy gets paid. He sells everything he finds."

"But he may not be able to dig much longer, especially
on public lands. You said yourself that the good relics have
gotten harder to find. If you studied archaeology, you could
work for a museum. And you could learn the history of the
Indian tribes that lived in Arkansas. Then you could teach
others about them."

"I can learn all I need to know from Roy Glen. He never
finished school, just seventh grade, and he knows a lot."

"I'm sure he does, and you could work with him in the
summer. Lots of students go into the field for some practical
experience on their summer vacations. Have you ever talked
to him about this—about dropping out of school and working with him?"

"Not much. I went down in the woods and found him
when Mama said she was leaving. He said I should stay
with my mama. I can't do that, Miss Criswell. I'd go crazy
stayin' in town all summer, never bein' in the woods. It's
not fair. Not fair fer her to do this to me." Tessa Mae had
forgotten about impressing Miss Criswell with her grammar.

"Your mother has to do what's right for her, Tessa Mae.

You happen to be caught in the middle of it."

Tessa Mae jumped up. "Why's everybody defendin' Mama? I need to do what's best for me, too. Why cain't I? Why cain't I decide what I want to do? She cain't make me live in town, can she?"

"When they go to court to get the divorce, a judge will decide where you have to live. Most likely he'll say you have to live with your mother. Children usually live with their mothers. But you're fourteen. He might—"

"Might what? Let me live with my daddy?" Tessa Mae saw a glimmer of hope.

"Let you choose. Let you have a say."

"He'd let me choose whether I wanted to live with my mama or my daddy? They wouldn't have no say?"

"*Any* say, Tessa Mae."

"Any say? My mama wouldn't have *any* say?"

"I'll tell you what, Tessa Mae." Miss Criswell finished the last of her tea, then set the empty glass back on the ground by a chair leg. "I'll make a deal with you."

"What's that?" Tessa Mae asked skeptically.

"I'll take you to Clarksville on Saturday to talk to a judge who's a friend of mine. Your mother's case probably won't come before him, but we'll see what he has to say. Your part of the bargain is that you come back and finish the school year."

Tessa Mae had walked right into a trap. It would be good to talk to this judge, but going back to school wouldn't be any fun. She could ignore her classmates, as usual. Trouble was, before, they had ignored her too. Now she was the subject of a lot of gossip, and some people—like Erline Crider—wouldn't hesitate to ask her questions. But what did Erline Crider count for anyway? Nothing at all. Tessa Mae looked at the young teacher who was smiling at her.

"Let's see, it's Thursday. I'll expect you in class on Monday morning. Deal?" Miss Criswell asked, holding out her hand.

"Deal." The teacher's hand was almost lost in Tessa Mae's. It felt soft, but her handshake was strong.

As Tessa Mae walked Miss Criswell back to her daddy's office, the cardinal started to sing more of his evening song. He echoed her new note of cheer. Miss Criswell's visit had given her some hope. It appeared that something might be done about her mother's insistence that she move to town.

Tessa Mae had tried running away. That usually didn't fix things. It sure hadn't this time. Now she'd go back—and fight.

CHAPTER

TWELVE

On Saturday morning at nine o'clock, Miss Criswell drove up into the yard.

"I brought you a dress." The teacher held out the red-striped seersucker. "I told your mother you were fine and what we were going to do. She didn't much like the idea, but she is worried about you, so she said you could go. I couldn't take you off without one parent's permission. You understand that, don't you?"

Tessa Mae nodded, then decided to get something off her mind. "Did my mama send you to see me on Thursday?" she asked.

"No she didn't, Tessa Mae. I came because I wanted to. I was worried about you and wanted to see if there was anything I could do."

"I don't want anyone worrying about me. I can take care of myself."

Miss Criswell didn't respond to Tessa Mae's declaration. Tessa Mae, still angry because she had a problem too big to take on alone, took the seersucker dress and changed. Then she climbed in the passenger side of the little blue Ford where Miss Criswell sat waiting. Without letting Miss Criswell see her doing it, she ran her fingers over the plush seats and the smooth navy blue leather of the interior. Miss Criswell pulled off the brake, shifted into reverse, and swung back out of the driveway.

Someday, Tessa Mae vowed, I'll have me a little old Ford— red, I'd like red. I'll drive into Lamar sittin' up tall for everyone to see. I'll drive right up to the house and smile at Roy Glen and say, "Hi there, Roy Glen. How're things goin' with you?" Roy Glen will grin and his eyes will bug out and then I'll say, "I reckon I'm doin' fine myself."

Miss Criswell turned off the highway, and Tessa Mae realized with a start that they were almost in Clarksville. Her stomach tightened as the realization of what she was going to do finally sank in: ask some judge, a total stranger, to help her with her life. It sounded like the worst idea she'd ever had. Of course, it wasn't her idea. It was Miss Criswell's idea, and Tessa Mae had let the teacher talk her into trying it.

She glanced at Miss Criswell. The teacher had on a white dress dotted with tiny blue flowers. Her sandals were the same shade of blue. Tessa Mae had never had shoes any other color than brown or black unless you counted the white on her saddle shoes. Miss Criswell was humming as she entered the city.

"The big city of Clarksville, ta-dah," she said. "Have you ever been to Little Rock, Tessa Mae?"

"I went there once with my daddy."

Clarksville wasn't anywhere near as big as Little Rock, Tessa Mae thought. It wasn't a whole lot bigger than Lamar.

The tree-bordered residential streets looked more prosperous than Lamar's. There was one main street, but it seemed to be about two miles long. As they drove down it, she spotted two movie theaters and a Sears, Roebuck, a Penney's department store and two five-and-dimes. Miss Criswell passed the courthouse and turned off onto a magnolia-bordered side street. Leaves from the magnolias littered the street, and the car crunched them as Miss Criswell pulled to the curb and stopped in front of a huge white frame house. A veranda ran all around the front and sides and comfortable-looking rattan couches and chairs beckoned them towards the shady front porch.

"This is where we're going, Tessa Mae. Let's get out." The teacher's voice had taken on a lilt as if she were delighted to be there. "Seems like a lot of house for one person, doesn't it?"

Tessa Mae had just assumed they'd go to a courthouse to see a judge, not a house. When Miss Criswell knocked, the door was opened by a tall black woman wearing a smart black dress with a snow white apron over it. Tessa Mae thought she must have had her hair styled in a beauty shop since it was cupped to her head in a fashionable way.

"Hello, Ruth," Miss Criswell said to the black woman. "Is the judge here? He was expecting us."

"Hi there, Miss Criswell." The woman opened the door wide. "You're lookin' mighty fresh for such a warm day. You come on in. I reckon the judge is workin' as usual. I don't understand a man who never even thinks of goin' fishin' on a Saturday mornin'."

Tessa Mae's legs felt shaky, and she longed to sit on the porch for a time to think about what she was doing. Miss Criswell acted as if they were paying a social call, but it was more like the teacher was taking her to the principal's office for playing hooky.

Miss Criswell said something to the housekeeper as she stepped inside the house, but Tessa Mae was too nervous to catch what it was. Automatically she followed the teacher into a cool, dimly lit hall and then to the back of the house. Miss Criswell seemed to know her way around. She knocked at a door, then opened it and went right in.

"Sharon, is it that late?" A tall, dark-haired man rose and came towards them. He wasn't elderly at all, the way Tessa Mae had imagined. He didn't have on a black robe, but khaki-colored slacks and a red shirt. He had eyes like Clark Gable's, and they sparkled as he looked at Miss Criswell. Tessa Mae was startled when he called her "Sharon" but then she realized that was Miss Criswell's first name.

"Ted," Miss Criswell said, turning to Tessa Mae. "I'd like you to meet my student, Tessa Mae Ferris."

Tessa Mae nodded.

"Tessa Mae, this is Judge Noble."

Tessa Mae's voice was gone. She didn't want it to squeak, so she just nodded again. He seemed to expect her to say something though. "H—howdy," she spoke and then bit her tongue. Educated people don't say "howdy," she knew. The judge would think she was a dumb kid from the country who could scarcely speak.

"Sit down, sit down." He was obviously trying to put her at ease. "Did you ask Ruth to bring us some ice tea, Sharon?"

"I sure did." Miss Criswell sat down in front of a large window, in a big overstuffed chair covered with dark green chintz. "She says you need to be out fishing instead of cooped up in here working." Miss Criswell and Judge Noble smiled at each other.

"Do you like to fish, Tessa Mae?" Judge Noble backed

up and sat in the swivel chair at his desk, swinging it around to face her.

She had perched on the edge of a hard chair by a table stacked with magazines and books. "Yes."

"Miss Criswell tells me you live on the edge of the woods. I'll bet you know where all the good fishing holes are."

"I reckon I do." Her mouth felt as dry as a parched stream bed in August. Darn! First "howdy." Now "reckon." Fortunately, they were interrupted by the housekeeper's return.

"You like yours with sugar, honey?" She handed Tessa Mae a tall flowered glass filled with amber tea. A slice of lemon floated on the top.

Tessa Mae nodded and spooned in two sugars while the tray was held for her. She wanted three but was embarrassed to take more. The glass was already sweating, and she grasped it with both hands. It would be horrible to spill it on the cream-colored rug. She glanced around while Judge Noble and Miss Criswell were being served.

The room was comfortable with many easy chairs, a couch, and three walls lined with books. A person could sit in any one of the chairs and read all day. Even so, it would take a couple of years to read all the books here. She guessed even the high school library didn't have so many.

The cold tea refreshed Tessa Mae's parched throat and mouth. She knew she was going to have to start talking soon.

"Sharon tells me you like to read, Tessa Mae," Judge Noble commented. "What are your favorite books?"

"I—I reckon . . . I like almost everything."

Miss Criswell laughed. "She's read almost every book in our classroom library, Ted, and a lot of mine."

"What else do you like to do with your summers?"

"Fish and mess around in the woods." She wanted to tell

the judge about looking for Indian relics but she couldn't seem to get any more words out than that.

"What do you want to do when you finish school, Tessa Mae?" the judge asked.

Before Tessa Mae could respond to the question that grown-ups loved to ask, Miss Criswell said, "She wants to be an archaeologist, Ted."

Even though Tessa Mae was having trouble talking, Miss Criswell didn't have any right answering for her. She'd never said she wanted to be something fancy like an archaeologist. That was Miss Criswell's idea. All Tessa Mae had said was that she'd like to dig out relics with Roy Glen.

"That's a fine ambition. Sharon—Miss Criswell—has told me a little about your problem, Tessa Mae. I'd like to hear what you have to say."

If Tessa Mae didn't speak now, Miss Criswell would have brought her all the way over here for nothing. She began slowly, trying to use proper grammar.

"It don't—doesn't—seem fair for you or some judge to decide who I should live with. How kin you know? It's not fair for my mama to run off to town and then expect me to go with her. I don't like livin' in town, and I want to live with my daddy. I should have some say since it's my life."

"Yes, I can understand how you feel, Tessa Mae. But sometimes adults can help a young person make better decisions about what is right, especially when she is mixed up and confused at the time."

"I'm not mixed up. I know what I want. My mama wants me to get a job and buy fancy clothes, but I want to work for my daddy, diggin' and helping him mail out his orders. I can learn a lot from him, and then if I did want to be an arche—archaeologist, I'd be way ahead of readin'—reading—what was in some books." She paused for breath and thought it a wonder that she'd said all that to the judge.

Judge Noble smiled. "You don't want any pretty clothes?"

"They'd get all muddy, digging in the river bottoms," she said, without smiling back.

To her surprise Tessa Mae found herself standing. She sat down quickly and looked at her hands, large and bony like her mother's.

The judge swiveled his chair around, his back to her, and scribbled on some papers at his desk, making Tessa Mae feel as if she had been dismissed. She glanced around the room, noting the huge windows that ran from floor to ceiling, framing leafy oak trees. Miss Criswell was standing at one of the windows, looking out.

Glancing at the books again, Tessa Mae longed to walk over and look at the titles, even handle them and turn their pages. Some were old. Each book would have a smell of its own, she knew.

"Tessa Mae." Judge Noble said, turning back to her. "I understand there are two more weeks of school. I have no legal say about this matter, but I'll call your mother's lawyer and suggest this agreement: You stay with your mother in town these two weeks and finish school. Then this summer you try living with your father, wherever he is staying. By fall the divorce case will come up and the court will have more background for making a permanent decision. And I promise you I'll talk it over with you before someone rules on it. Does this seem fair?"

Tessa Mae tried to grasp all he was saying. "I reckon— I *think*—it does."

"You understand your mother and your father have to agree on this arrangement? Your father has to approve of your coming to live with him this summer?"

"He will. I know he will," Tessa Mae answered firmly.

"Feel free to look at the books, Tessa Mae." Judge Noble must have seen her gazing at them. She walked over to the bookshelves, but she was too excited about living with her daddy to look at books now. Maybe, just maybe, her luck had come back.

"Thanks, Ted." Miss Criswell walked over to the judge and smiled at him. "I'll see you later."

Relieved that the meeting was over, Tessa Mae quickly left the bookshelves, gave the judge a polite "thank you," and practically ran out of the room ahead of Miss Criswell.

Bursting out the front screen door onto the porch, she took a deep breath. A robin chortled from the row of magnolias beside the car, and Tessa Mae felt like whistling back the musical notes. Three months. She had three months to put everything right.

"Well now, Tessa Mae. What shall we do?" Miss Criswell asked when they were in the car. "As long as we're in the big city, we might as well enjoy its offerings."

Although Miss Criswell was teasing about Clarksville being a big city, to Tessa Mae it was. She loved her woods the best, but it was still different and exciting to be here. Especially with Miss Criswell. But now that their business was over, she felt awkward with the young teacher. Miss Criswell had entered the judge's house casually, and called him Ted instead of Judge Noble. It wasn't hard to figure out where Miss Criswell went every Saturday, or that today she'd changed her usual plans to include Tessa Mae. As they walked to the car, Tessa Mae said,

"I—I—I could catch a bus home if you want to—want to—"

"Want to what?" Miss Criswell smiled her June Allyson smile.

"Well, you know. Maybe you'd like to be with some of your . . . friends, and now I'm in the way."

"If you mean Judge Noble, Tessa Mae, I'll see him later. Don't worry, you certainly aren't in the way. I like to think you're my friend too. Friends help each other out. I wanted to see if Ted could help you and I think he can. I'm glad for that." The teacher's smile put Tessa Mae back at ease.

"I reck—I believe—he can too."

Miss Criswell started the car, turned around, and headed back downtown. As they passed the Clarksville Criterion theater, she said, "Oh, look, Tessa Mae, they're playing *Saratoga Trunk* with Ingrid Bergman and Gary Cooper. Let's go to the movie. We'll have lunch first. My treat. Want to?"

Tessa Mae nearly always went to the movies alone. Going with Miss Criswell sounded like the most fun she'd had in a long time. At the counter at Walgreen's Drug Store, Miss Criswell ordered a tuna salad sandwich, but Tessa Mae got that too often at home. She chose a grilled cheese. While they waited for their food, Tessa Mae watched the girls in their pink striped uniforms behind the counter, wondering if they liked working there. Miss Criswell's mind had wandered off somewhere, and Tessa Mae didn't want to interrupt her thinking.

The grilled cheese came, golden with butter on the outside, and melted cheese oozing out the sides. She enjoyed every bite, sipping her Coke to wash it down.

Tessa Mae had never had a girl friend. Sometimes she watched girls at her school as they left together, arms around each other, or more often teasing and laughing, poking and pushing and giggling. Sometimes she yearned for that kind of friendship, yet it didn't seem it would come naturally to her. Even in grade school she had hung back, joining only in games of ball and chase, active games where she could take part without belonging to the crowd.

This was the first time in her life she'd ever sat and eaten with a woman who was not part of her family or Jec's.

Suddenly she was bursting with the need to share some secrets with Miss Criswell, to talk to her as she would Jec. The pretty teacher knew more about her life than almost anyone else and hadn't laughed at her or criticized her yet.

"I know you probably think I don't have any friends, Miss Criswell," she began, "but I do. He's not in my school, but . . ."

A torrent of words flooded out of Tessa Mae. She told Miss Criswell about Jec and the Browns and the fish fry and the Wednesday night prayer meeting. "I wish I could be a part of a big family like that," she confessed.

Miss Criswell didn't seem shocked by Tessa Mae's friendship with Jec and his family. She was quiet for a moment, accepting Tessa Mae's gift of sharing. Then she answered. "I wish I could too, Tessa Mae. When I get married I'm going to have a big family. I was an only child. My father died when I was very young and my mother is ill now. I always wished I was one of ten kids."

It was a wonder to Tessa Mae that she and Miss Criswell could have many of the same feelings, the same longings. Tessa Mae decided to share one more thing with Miss Criswell to see how she felt about it.

"I think until now I figured all adults were doing just what they wanted to do with their lives. But I guess my mama's not or she wouldn't go off and get a divorce. I guess that's really what she wants to do. Did you ever know anyone who got a divorce, Miss Criswell?"

Miss Criswell thought a minute. "Yes, but I didn't know her well."

"I don't think I'll ever get married. There's too many problems and how could you know it'd work out? I figure it'd be easier to go off and live alone like Thoreau."

"It might be easier, Tessa Mae, but life would be awfully

lonely if we all decided to keep to ourselves. There's a lot of risk involved with loving someone and deciding to get married. But there's risk involved with everything we choose to do. There are never any guarantees for happiness. It wasn't easy for me to risk leaving my home and coming here to teach. I didn't know anyone in Lamar or Clarksville. Little Rock had always been my home. But if I hadn't risked leaving home, I'd never have met Ted."

Miss Criswell gently put her hand over Tessa Mae's. "It'll take a lot of courage for you to work out the problems your parents are giving you just now. But you have that courage, Tessa Mae. I've seen it in you, courage and the intelligence I've admired. You have to let your parents live their own lives and keep loving them no matter what they do or say— or even don't say—to you."

"My mama keeps sayin' she loves me, but how could she do this to me if she does?"

"She's not doing something to you, Tessa Mae. She's doing something *for* herself. And I'd guess it was a hard decision for her to make. Especially living in a little town like Lamar where everyone knows everybody else's problems and loves to gossip about them. I'd also guess that she needs to know you love her right now more than she ever has."

Tessa Mae hadn't sorted out her feelings about her mother, but it didn't seem likely that Mama needed her to say she loved her.

Miss Criswell kept her hand on Tessa Mae's and kept talking. "And don't let your parents' divorce make you decide you won't ever get married, Tessa Mae. Someday you'll fall in love with someone and he'll fall in love with you, and that's a very special thing to happen. You'll have to have the courage to keep loving him no matter how scary it is. Can you keep a secret, Tessa Mae? A big one?"

"Sure I can. I have lots of secrets inside me." Tessa Mae looked at Miss Criswell, who was beaming.

"I'm going to be married this summer, probably in August. After summer school is over."

"To Judge Noble?"

"You already knew, didn't you? You're a very sensitive and perceptive person, Tessa Mae. Or else my face always gives me away. I think it's probably a combination of both." She laughed, savoring the joke.

"I'm real pleased for you, Miss Criswell. I like the judge." She was especially pleased that Miss Criswell chose to trust her with her secret.

"So do I, and I'm glad to have a friend to share my secret with. I was about to pop with thinking about it today. I'm not ready to tell anyone at school, although I'll probably not be back next year. I'll teach in Clarksville. Hey, we'd better go. The movie starts in fifteen minutes."

The movie theater was close by. Tessa Mae thought about Miss Criswell and Judge Noble all through the picture, especially during the love scenes with Gary Cooper and Miss Ingrid Bergman. She wondered if she'd ever fall in love. Miss Criswell had said it was a risk and took courage to love someone. In the movies and in some of the books she'd read, love and marriage were like fairy tales in which people lived happily ever after. Her mother and daddy's separation had proved real life was different.

That knowledge made her feel she'd lost something. Now there was an empty place inside her, but she didn't have anything, not even her new friendship with Miss Criswell, to put in its place. As the images faded from the screen, Tessa Mae took a deep breath and prayed she'd find some of that courage Miss Criswell thought she had pretty soon.

CHAPTER
THIRTEEN

After the movie Miss Criswell drove Tessa Mae home. She waited while Tessa Mae gathered her books and her gym shorts, then dropped her off at the little house in town.

"See you Monday?" Miss Criswell said as Tessa Mae got out of the car.

"Yes, sure," Tessa Mae replied. "It was a deal. And thanks. I'm grateful to you."

The teacher smiled and drove off. Tessa Mae waited until the car was out of sight; then walked slowly towards the house. She was hesitating outside the door when her mother opened it. Mama had on a new dress, black with pink roses. Pink ruffles edged the sleeves and collar. It was a party dress, and Tessa Mae wondered if her mother was going someplace or just getting back. When Mama hugged her, Tessa Mae could smell her sweet lilac perfume. Tessa Mae felt awkward in her mother's embrace, but at least she hadn't started to scold her right away.

Finally Tessa Mae pulled away and walked past her mother into the house. "That's a pretty new dress. Are you going somewhere, Mama?"

"No place, Tessa Mae. No place at all. I was just sittin' here, listenin' to the radio, hopin' you'd come home tonight. That teacher is a nice lady, ain't she?"

"Yes. We went to the movie in Clarksville. It's a new one with Gary Cooper. You should get Dixie Lee to take you over to see it."

"Maybe I will next weekend. Did you . . . Did you see that judge?" Her mother was still trying to smile, but she looked anxious.

"I'm goin' to stay here and finish the school year, Mama. Then I'm goin' to go live with Roy Glen all summer." Tessa Mae didn't mention anything about her parents having to agree to this arrangement. Maybe her mother would think it was the law already.

"I don't understand you wantin' to do that, Tessa Mae. I thought you liked livin' in town. Part of the reason I made this change was fer you. So you could have a normal life. What fun could that be fer a girl, campin' down on the river?" Her mother's voice started to get shrill.

"I like doin' that, Mama," Tessa Mae insisted, feeling her stomach tighten back up like it did lately when she had to be with her mother. "I like camping on the river, bein' in the woods. I like watchin' the animals and helpin' Roy Glen dig for Indian relics." Tessa Mae didn't want to fight. She'd had too good a day, a special day with Miss Criswell, and she was determined to keep her promise not to run away again. "What's to drink, Mama? Did you ever have time to get in some groceries?"

"Course I did." Her mama seemed relieved to change the subject, too. "There's R.C. Cola and some Nehi orange and a couple of Grapettes. All your favorites."

Tessa Mae put her belongings in her room, then took a Grapette from the refrigerator, savoring the sweet flavor.

"I got us some chicken to fry for supper." Her mother stood by the sink watching her. "And I'll make gravy like you favor. I know you haven't been eatin' right."

"I had supper at Bertha's a couple of times. We had catfish one night."

"Did you have hush puppies or corn bread?" Mama asked. "Bertha makes the best corn bread in town."

"We had hush puppies, but I'll get her to show me how to make her corn bread if you want me to," Tessa Mae offered.

"That's a good idea. You need to be learning to cook better."

Tessa Mae headed for her room, intending to shut the door until supper. She wanted to write in her notebook diary. But when she walked out of the kitchen, her mother followed her, right into the bedroom. Tessa Mae stood uncomfortably. It was almost easier when Mama fussed. At least Tessa Mae knew how to handle that. This friendly woman in the pretty dress frightened her.

"Did you notice how I brought your curtains and fixed up yer room some?" Mama asked, sitting down in a straight-backed chair like she planned to stay awhile.

"Yes I did. It looks more homey." Tessa Mae noticed there was a curtain at her window, a rug on the floor, and Grandma Ferris's double wedding ring quilt on the bed. Tessa Mae pulled off her dress and hung it up, hoping it wasn't too dirty to wear again. Her calico dresses were practically rags.

"When I went shoppin' today, fer myself, I also looked at dresses for young ladies," her mama said, practically reading her thoughts. "Somethin' besides those old cotton dresses to finish out the school year. And I found one that will do till fall when we'll shop for a lot of new clothes. I tell you what." Her mama stood up. "You jist slip that new dress on. I'm goin' to start supper. When you get ready you come and let me see how it fits, you hear?"

Tessa Mae didn't answer. She sat on the bed, sipping her grape drink and watched her mother leave the room. Mama had gone to a lot of trouble while she'd been away, and that started to make her feel better in spite of herself. Her mother hadn't been this nice in a long time. She looked rested, too, and pretty in the black and pink dress.

The new dress was hanging in the closet. It was robin's egg blue, one of Tessa Mae's favorite colors. She stared at it for a minute, then slipped it off the hanger. The style was similar to the seersucker with a dropped waist and the skirt hanging in small pleats all the way around. There was a wide band around the top of the pleats and white buttons were spaced on the band for decoration. The bodice fit loosely, hiding the figure she wasn't yet entirely comfortable with.

Tessa Mae ran her hands down the sides of the dress, enjoying the smooth, polished feel of it and the smell of the new material. According to the full length mirror fastened on the closet door, the color made her hair look even redder. While Tessa Mae didn't consider herself pretty, there seemed to be some improvement since the last time she looked. Her mama had chosen a pretty dress this time, one that Tessa Mae might have chosen for herself.

She walked to the kitchen. "Thanks for the dress, Mama. It's real pretty."

"Why, you look beautiful, honey. I jist knew it'd suit you

the very minute I saw it." Mama beamed, her cheeks red from the heat of the kitchen, her eyes sparkling as she looked Tessa Mae over, turning her round and round. "You want to get your hair cut for summer? With it curlin' all natural like, it'd be pretty short and fluffy around your face."

"No, Mama. I like it this way." Suddenly Tessa Mae felt the urge to escape before her mother got control over her life again. She went to her room, pulled off the dress, and put her shorts back on.

On Monday Tessa Mae timed her arrival at school so that the bell rang just as she came in the classroom door. She was wearing the new blue dress. Miss Criswell called the class to order right away, nodding and smiling at Tessa Mae, without doing or saying anything to indicate their new friendship. Tessa Mae was happy to have it a private feeling between them.

The two weeks flew by. Each day Tessa Mae slipped in just after the bell, went home for lunch, and generally kept to herself. As her classmates started to get excited about summer, they forgot about Tessa Mae. Only rarely did the warm afternoons prompt her to stare out the window and wish she was in the woods. The classroom fairly hummed with activity, and preparations for exams and reports kept her busy at night. Sometimes she listened to the radio while she studied, but more often she went to her room. There was an agreed and almost comfortable silence between her and her mother.

She missed Jec, but didn't have time to go looking for him. And she was afraid that once she made it back to the woods, she'd want to stay. She visited Elbert and Maudie as often as she could. Roy Glen had told them about the divorce, and Maudie said it was a shame, but she thought

Vinnie had a right to do what she wanted, especially if she wasn't happy.

Two days before school let out, Mama got home early. She and Tessa Mae were fixing dinner together, Tessa Mae peeling potatoes to chop and fry, her mother making meat-loaf.

"Have you seen Roy Glen lately, Mama?" Tessa Mae asked.

"No, I reckon he's busy." Mama stirred egg and chopped onion into the ground beef and pork meat. "Tessa Mae, you know I don't want you to stay down there all summer. It's not proper for a girl your age. What's people goin' to think about you campin' out and diggin' around like . . . like . . . Well, it jist ain't proper."

"Archaeologists do it all the time." Tessa Mae had done some reading about archaeologists and their work. Maybe her mother would feel better if she knew that many people thought what she and Roy Glen were doing was proper. "They go all over the world, campin' at sites where people once lived. They dig up relics and learn about those people. They kin tell what a whole ancient civilization was like jist by the few things they find."

"That teacher has put fancy ideas into your head. I never heard of such a thing. Just because your daddy does such foolishness is no reason fer you to do the same. It jist ain't proper."

"Even the judge said it was a fine ambition," Tessa Mae added.

Mama thought about that for a moment. "I don't care, Tessa Mae. I want you here. I—I'll miss you. I love you and I want you to stay here with me. You kin get a job and buy some clothes fer school. You cain't start ninth grade with only two dresses."

Tessa Mae had heard only one thing her mother had said, but it gave her the courage to blurt out the questions she'd been longing to ask. "Mama, if you love me, why did you leave Roy Glen and move to town? Why did you mess up our family? We could have all been really happy jist like we was."

Her mother looked startled at Tessa Mae's outburst. "I— I wasn't happy no more. And because I left your daddy don't mean I don't love you. You should know that."

"You mean you just don't love Roy Glen anymore?"

"No." Mama's voice broke. "I love your daddy, too, Tessa Mae. I just cain't live with his drinkin' and foolishness. His daydreamin' and goin' off all the time diggin' after rocks and broken pots and—"

"You knew he went off diggin' Indian relics when you married him, Mama. Why did you marry him?"

Her mother hesitated before she answered. "'Cause I loved him. And . . . well . . . It seemed kinda romantic to me what he did then, not sittin' in town sellin' shoes or somethin' like everyone else. I was too young to understand that a proper job and money coming in regular is much better. I even went campin' with him a couple of times. He showed me what he found and how happy he was to find it. Then it got rainy and campin' wasn't no fun anymore. Next I got pregnant with you, and I was lonely sittin' there in that house by myself all the time. Sometimes I'd go two weeks without seein' Roy Glen or knowin' where he was. I didn't know no one in town, not bein' from Lamar, and I had a little baby and couldn't go no place by myself. Then he'd come in all excited about what he'd found and I was supposed to get excited, too. About some broken pieces of pottery dishes or old dirty rocks."

"But that was history, Mama. He was diggin' history out of the ground. That *is* excitin'."

"I don't care. He could have left it buried fer all I cared. Oh, you wouldn't understand, Tessa Mae. You're jist like him." Tears rolled down her mother's cheeks. Tessa Mae looked away, but she kept on talking.

"Then how kin you love me, Mama, if I'm jist like Roy Glen? How kin you want me around?" Tessa Mae stared at the potato she'd been peeling and slipped her knife under another curl of skin. "I'd think you'd be glad to git rid of me, too."

Her mother was crying even harder, frightening Tessa Mae. She was tempted to put her arms around her mother and tell her not to cry, but she didn't. She couldn't. She could start crying too, and then her mother might think she was giving in about the summer.

"Then go on." Her mama pressed the meatloaf mixture into a pan, her mouth hardening. "Go on down there and live with him if he'll have you. Dig up all that old stuff— dig up half of Arkansas if you want. Let people laugh and make fun of you. I don't even care no more." Mama wiped her eyes and blew her nose on her hankerchief, then put the meatloaf in the oven. Saying nothing more, she walked out the front door and down the street towards Dixie Lee's.

Tessa Mae finished cooking the supper, but she didn't feel much like eating. She sat at the kitchen table, her food untouched, pondering the days ahead. School was pretty much over. Tomorrow they'd clean out their desks and help straighten the room. The day after that, report cards would be handed out. She knew she'd passed. There was really no reason for her to return to the school at all. She could write a note to Miss Criswell saying that she hoped the teacher would have a good summer and that all her plans went well. Miss Criswell would know what Tessa Mae meant. By noon tomorrow she could be with Roy Glen.

She moved about the kitchen, clearing away the dishes,

wondering if her mother had done her a favor by leaving Roy Glen. Tessa Mae had been unhappy over it, but maybe now her life was going to change in a way she never could have imagined. Her mother had said she didn't care anymore, so that meant Tessa Mae was free—free to live as she pleased. She'd dress as she pleased and talk as she pleased. There wouldn't be anyone around to say, "What will people think?" She would visit her mother when they came to town to get the mail or supplies, of course, but she wouldn't stay long enough for Mama to start telling her what to do.

All this spring she had wished she could go back in time, be the carefree person she had been last summer, and now it seemed as if that wish were coming true. But it was going to be even better, since she wouldn't ever have to explain where she'd been or why she liked being so free. It was only after she'd heard her mother come in that she could get her thoughts to settle down. Moonlight streamed in her window, and in Tessa Mae's optimistic mood, she imagined that it was lighting up her future.

CHAPTER
FOURTEEN

After Tessa Mae's two weeks in town, the woods looked even better to her. Oak and hickory trees were thickly leafed out, their new spring green contrasting with the dark emerald of the cedar and pine. She stopped to admire a persimmon tree whose trunk was garnished with orange fungus and pale gray lichen. A graceful dogwood bent towards her, heavy with the leaves of approaching summer. The fragrance of its blossoms lingered, and she breathed deeply of the air, seasoned with the scents of spring's finale.

She had fought her yearning to flee to the house she loved, knowing it sat empty as if waiting for her return. She'd pretended that living in town was a sentence she'd got for running off, for playing hooky from school.

Now she was finally free. She could stay where she felt loved and safe. The woods symbolized safety, a warm robe of acceptance that she had wrapped around her since she was a child. Roy Glen didn't know she was coming to live with him, but she tried not to worry about that, tried to forget about his saying, "Go back to town, you cain't live with me."

She inspected the house for signs of him, but he hadn't been around. Mail was piled up in an Indian basket on his desk. Folks who ordered from Roy Glen had to have a lot of patience. They'd get an answer in time, but not as fast as from the Sears catalogue.

She had stopped at Miller's grocery store to get peanut butter and crackers, candy bars and cookies. Roy Glen would have some supplies, of course, but she wanted to be prepared. Now she repacked her bedroll, tossing in her knife and her notebook, a long-sleeved shirt in case it got cool or the mosquitoes swarmed too thickly. A person didn't need much camping out, and you could always come to town when you ran out of necessary items. Slamming the porch door behind her, she set out on her trek.

About a mile down the path she stopped to put on her shoes. She'd go barefoot all summer as soon as her feet toughened up, unless they had to walk a long way where there were lots of snakes.

It was past lunchtime when she stopped by a sweet-smelling honeysuckle bush to eat the bologna and cheese sandwich she'd brought from town. Mama had already left for work when Tessa Mae set out, supposedly for school. She'd planned it that way so she wouldn't have to argue anymore about the summer. She'd just packed a lunch and left a note that said she'd stop by when she and Roy Glen were in town.

Tessa Mae felt fine sitting there on a log eating her lunch. Even though she hadn't found her daddy, she still felt fine.

Maybe she was a person who was meant to live alone, she reflected. God had planned for many animals to live alone most of the time: mountain lions and black bears and snakes. Roy Glen liked being alone. Even when he was with Tessa Mae and Mama, he was mostly alone. Being by herself didn't scare Tessa Mae nearly as much as going off to high school or college in a strange place with strange people.

The gray-and-white flash of a mockingbird sailed by. A wood thrush whistled his fine song. Who was alone? Tessa Mae happily looked around her. There was plenty of company here.

Still, she didn't want to camp by herself that night unless she had to—not when she'd set her sights on finding Roy Glen. It had been nearly three weeks since she'd seen him. Sometimes, when the family was together, he'd go a long ways off and she wouldn't see him for a week or more. But this was different.

She carefully folded up the waxed paper from her sandwich, in case it came in handy and saved the Hershey Bar wrapper to put on the fire that night.

It was late afternoon when she came across his camp. She found it accidently after trying every place she knew. This was a new spot, but it lay between a camp near the river and the last one Tessa Mae could remember, way back under some cliffs. She trudged towards the limestone outcroppings, resigned to camping alone, when she spotted a dead campfire in a clearing. Roy Glen's battered and blackened camping coffee pot rested on a flat rock.

She smiled, and tired and thirsty as she was, threw down her gear and went to look for his actual digging spot. She found him resting near a pile of dug-out rocks and shells.

"Hey there, Roy Glen," she said casually and grinned. "Ain't it about suppertime?"

He jumped up, surprised, and stared as if he didn't know her. Without thinking, she ran to him and hugged him. He kept his body stiff and didn't put his arms around her. She didn't care. It felt wonderful to be near him.

"What are you doin' here, Tessa Mae?" It was the same thing he'd asked her before, but in a different tone of voice.

"This judge in Clarksville said that if I'd stay with Mama and finish school, I could come live with you all summer," Tessa Mae said quickly. "Ain't that fine?"

"A judge told you that?" Roy Glen mused over the idea. "Your mama's already been to court?"

"No, Mama wasn't there. I went to see him myself. My teacher took me. I told the judge that it wasn't fair that I had to go and live in town, and he said I could try living with you. That is, if you say it's all right."

"You cain't live out here in the woods, Tessa Mae. It's not proper for a girl." Roy Glen took off his hat and ran his hand through his hair.

Tessa Mae took a deep beath before saying, "Roy Glen, if you don't want me here with you, say so. Don't lay it onto being proper. You look me right in the eye and say, 'Tessa Mae, I don't want you here with me,' and I'll go away. But I'll not spend the summer in town, you hear? I'll live by myself somewhere. So you jist tell me you don't love me and I'll git out."

Roy Glen sat down. His gray eyes were clear and he looked rested, much better than the last time Tessa Mae had seen him. First he stared at his cigarette and took another puff. Then he looked at Tessa Mae.

"Well, I reckon it would be all right to stay here a few days, Tessa Mae. As long as your mama knows where you are and says it's okay."

"She knows where I am but she ain't happy about it. I

told her I was comin' anyway. And not fer a few days. All summer, Roy Glen. All summer." Tessa Mae was practically shouting. "Will you jist fer once ferget what Mama wants or thinks and listen to what I want? I want to stay down here with you and dig and learn all I can about what you're doin'. That way if I decide to do it for a livin', I'll already have a head start on knowing how."

Roy Glen seemed to be mulling over what she'd said. Then he looked at her and grinned. "Well, I reckon if you feel that strong about it, then you'd better do it."

"Oh, Daddy." She sat beside him on the rock and put her arm around his shoulders, hugging him. He smelled of tobacco and dusty limestone rock. She could tell her gesture of affection embarrassed him, but he didn't push her away. It would be wonderful if he could say right out that he loved her and that he wanted her to stay. But since he couldn't, she'd just have to believe it was true.

"Went to see a judge, did you?" Roy Glen mumbled and chuckled to himself. He finished his cigarette in a comfortable silence and then stood up. "I reckon it's about suppertime. Are you hungry?"

"Starved," Tessa Mae said with a smile. Suddenly, everything was going to be all right after all.

But when they came back to the small camp, Tessa Mae saw what she'd missed in her excitement at finding Roy Glen. There was a second bedroll beside the fire and a fancy pack of gear leaned up against the huge oak that shaded their site.

Before she could ask whose they were, a young man stepped into the clearing with two fine spear points spread on his palm. "Look what I found, Roy Glen." His eyes traveled from Roy Glen to Tessa Mae in about the time it would take a lightning bug to flicker off and on. He blinked his blue eyes as if she were a ghost. Then he smiled, making Tessa Mae feel funny all deep inside. It was a smile she knew but couldn't quite place. Then she remembered—Van Johnson, one of her favorite movie stars, had a smile like that, teasing and grinning at the same time.

"Looks like you had better luck than I did, though, Roy Glen," he said in perfect grammar. "Who is this? Some long-lost Indian princess?"

CHAPTER
FIFTEEN

Indian princess? Tessa Mae giggled despite her surprise.

"This here's my daughter, Guy. Looks like she's goin' to be stayin' awhile. I don't know what the attraction is down here in these woods, but if any more decide to move into our camp it's goin' to get mighty overpopulated."

The boy named Guy looked at Tessa Mae for a while longer before he said hello. Then he went back to telling Roy Glen where he'd found the spear points, sounding a lot like Miss Criswell, making no effort to include Tessa Mae. Roy Glen seemed to forget she was there, too, and when Guy asked him to examine the new digging site, they walked off together.

"Stir up that fire and put some water on to boil, will you, Tessa Mae?" Roy Glen called to her as he left. Slamming the pot down, she resentfully did what he asked. She'd come to live with her daddy, not her daddy and some boy she didn't even know. What right did he have to be there? Roy Glen was her daddy, not his.

Tessa Mae had no intention of cooking supper while they dug for relics. She was planning to dig alongside Roy Glen, and right now she wanted to see the new site, too. Resolutely she headed after them, up a shady path towards a stream that fed the river, until she realized she didn't feel comfortable running after her daddy and that boy like she would after Jec. How old is Guy? she wondered. He wasn't from Lamar. He was so good-looking she knew she'd remember if she had ever seen him.

Feeling like Jane Wyman in *My Favorite Spy*, she sneaked quietly down through the woods until she glimpsed Roy Glen's red-and-black checkered shirt. She'd crouched behind a small, shaggy cedar tree when a red squirrel spotted her and chattered loudly. Fortunately Roy Glen and Guy were too absorbed in their find to wonder why the squirrel was raising such a fuss. They were both on their knees, scratching at the bank of sand that bordered a long-discarded arm of the river.

Tessa Mae watched Guy closely. His hair was the light brown color of hickory nuts and shone in the last rays of the sun as if he'd just washed it. He wore it long, or else he needed a haircut badly. Most of the boys in Lamar had crew cuts. Van Johnson had a crew cut in his last movie, but Tessa Mae figured that his hair might look like Guy's if he let it grow out.

Suddenly she felt silly crouching there, spying. She got to her feet quietly and headed back to start supper. She was hungry, too.

The water was boiling by the time she found the big iron skillet, opened a can of Spam, and sliced it with her pocket knife. It smelled good frying, and the sizzling sound mixed with the song of a cicada announcing that evening was coming fast. Dumping some coffee in the pot of water, she placed it on a rock near the flames to keep it warm. A can of baked beans and one of peaches would round out the meal.

"That smells good, Tessa Mae." Roy Glen stepped into the camp circle, followed by Guy, whose eyes met Tessa Mae's. He smiled at her again.

"Sure does." Guy echoed Roy Glen's words and dug a tin cup out of his pack. "Thanks, Tessa Mae. It was my turn to cook. I'll get breakfast." He poured a cup of cold water into the coffee to settle the grounds and then helped himself to a cup. He watched Tessa Mae as she dished up three plates of food, making her feel clumsy and nervous. She had never paid much attention to boys, and she didn't want to now. But he was there, looking at her. The food stuck in her throat, and she kept washing it down with coffee.

Guy insisted on doing the dishes, so he gathered the plates and skillet, took a flashlight, and headed for the river.

"Where'd that boy come from, Roy Glen?" Tessa Mae asked when he was out of sight. "How long is he goin' to stay?"

"He showed up here one day last week. Said he'd spent a lot of time lookin' fer me. 'Pears he's gettin' some fancy degree up at the university, but said he wanted some practical experience, diggin' for relics."

"He was lookin' for relics, or lookin' fer you?" Tessa Mae watched Roy Glen shake tobacco from a small muslin sack onto a cigarette paper and roll it up.

"Lookin' for me. Ain't that a wonder?" Roy Glen picked a loose shred of tobacco off his tongue. "Said his professor told him about where I might be." He smoked quietly for a moment. "How's yer mama, Tessa Mae?"

Tessa Mae didn't want to talk about her mama, but Roy

Glen had brought it up. "She's fine. But I've been doin' a lot of thinkin' on what's happened, Roy Glen. Why did Mama go off like she did?"

Roy Glen poked at the fire until it flared. Then he set the coffee pot on it again. "I've never tried to tell your mama what to do, Tessa Mae. She has a mind of her own, a powerful strong way with her. You know that. It's the same way you've got, goin' to see some judge in Clarksville, then comin' down here against yer mama's thinkin'.."

"But if you'd have asked her to stay—"

"She might be happy in town. Not much has made her happy for a long time." Roy Glen's voice was wistful. "I cain't change to suit her, and she's got her mind set on things bein' different. Let her be."

"Is that what you want?"

"I reckon."

Tessa Mae found it hard to understand her daddy's thinking. He seemed resigned to letting her mother make all the decisions about their family. Maybe he'd never had much fight inside. He sure wasn't going to put up a fight for Tessa Mae. It seemed he let his life meander like a river, following a path of least resistance. If that was the way Roy Glen chose, she couldn't fault him for it. But it wasn't her way. She wanted to be in charge of her life.

Guy's footsteps interrupted her thoughts. She glanced at him as he sat down near the fire, wondering how long he was going to stay. But it soon became obvious that Roy Glen enjoyed having a new audience for his stories. Guy began asking questions about Roy Glen's work, and Roy Glen told some tales that Tessa Mae had heard before. She never got tired of them, though, so she got comfortable and listened. Her favorite, the one she'd heard the most, was about a skeleton that Roy Glen had found in a cave, holding

on to a Civil War rifle as if even in death it was going to
fight.

Roy Glen had sold that Civil War rifle three times. Tessa
Mae had been in his office when one customer stopped by,
heard the story, and bought the rifle on the spot. Then
twice more she'd seen Roy Glen mail similar rifles, each
with a letter attached, telling the same story. Tessa Mae
smiled and sipped her second cup of sweet, muddy coffee.
If Guy were a customer she'd make a bet he'd buy that gun
right now.

Watching them, listening, she resolved not to be resent-
ful. Guy's presence at the camp seemed good for Roy Glen.
The one thing her daddy liked as much as digging was
telling stories about his finds. Tessa Mae could see that it
helped him to have a fresh audience. He laughed and ges-
tured, happier than he'd been in a long time.

So Tessa Mae decided she would put up with Guy, even
use her best grammar when he was around. She'd do it for
Roy Glen's sake.

When her father announced he was turning in, Tessa Mae
slipped down to the river with her toothbrush, a wash cloth,
and a few personal items. She'd meant to wash up quickly
and then roll into her blanket, but the coffee had got her
wide awake. She sat on the riverbank for a time, letting
the quiet murmur of the water fill her with peace. When
she returned to camp, Guy had stirred the fire to a small
blaze. He sat staring into it as she had stared at the river.

She sat on the opposite side of the campfire and asked,
"How long are you going to stay here with Roy Glen, Guy?"
The words had slipped right out, and she tried to soften
them with a smile.

Guy looked at her and grinned. "You want me to leave?
I had a feeling you weren't too happy to find me here."

"I—I—" She stammered. "I just wondered—well—what you were doin'—doin*g*—here to begin with. How did you even know to come here looking for Roy Glen?"

"One of my teachers at the university buys arrowheads from your father. He told me about Roy Glen and how he's been digging for Indian relics down here for years and years. I decided I could learn from him if he'd let me stay here for a couple of months."

If Guy was going to stay that long, Tessa Mae had better get used to him. "I can't believe you heard about my daddy at the University of Arkansas," she said.

"He's pretty well known by my professors. He sells spears and arrowheads to the museum. All of these relics he finds should go into the collections there, but they can't stop him from digging on private land."

"Are there people who want to stop Roy Glen from digging out the Indian relics?" Tessa Mae remembered Miss Criswell saying a similar thing.

"The Indians that lived here are very much a part of Arkansas history. Their remains, their relics, should be preserved. At least . . ." Guy smiled. "That's what my professors say."

"Who would dig up these relics if my daddy didn't do it?"

"Archaeologists from the college—with students helping. Since your father knows the area so well, he could help in a way no one else could. He could be a guide for teams in the field. They'd pay him for his time and for teaching students what he knew."

"Is that what you're studying at school—archaeology?" Tessa Mae stared at Guy. His eyes were shining with excitement. It was his smile that had made his eyes light up. Now, with his serious mood, he looked older and not so boyish.

"Yes. Right now I want to dig in Arkansas and maybe Colorado or Arizona. But someday I want to go all over the world. There's important work being done in Africa. I'd like to be a part of it." He grinned again. "Does that sound silly?"

"My daddy teaching for the university sounds silly, even if he taught here in the woods. I reckon—I feel—your plans aren't so far fetched. I've thought some on it myself. But I figure digging with Roy Glen I'll learn about as much or more than you will from a bunch of books."

"You can learn the practical side of taking out relics, that's true. That's why I came out here, to make sure I like doing this, in addition to studying about it." He paused and looked at her until she had to look away. "You know, there aren't many girls in my class. Not many girls are willing to work in the field. Have you been coming down here with Roy Glen all your life?"

"I come down here when I can. Now I'm fixing—I mean, I'm planning—to dig with Roy Glen all summer. I don't need a bed when I've got a blanket and some moss or leaves. The ground isn't hard here on the bottoms."

"You're certainly independent, aren't you? I admire a girl who can adapt to the out-of-doors so easily."

No boy had ever said he admired her. Living outside was so natural for her, she had never thought it was anything special. "I feel more comfortable out here than I do anywhere else. People make fun of me at school." Vexed, she stirred the fire and fell silent. Words seemed to get away easily when she was talking to Guy.

He didn't laugh. "Because you like being here in the woods?"

She shrugged. "And because I like to be alone, and my mother and daddy are getting a divorce." She ducked her head and studied her toes. She'd said it all now, told him her problems, and she didn't even know why.

He poked at the coals with a hickory stick. There was enough light from the fire to see that his face was more serious than ever.

"My classmates laughed at me, too, sometimes. They didn't understand my wanting to dig in the dirt all my life. Maybe there are more glamorous careers and maybe ones where I'd make more money, but for me, there's so much excitement about archaeology."

Tessa Mae felt that way too. Digging was always a kind of treasure hunt. Now she was glad she'd shared a piece of what she was like, deep inside, because he'd given it back. "What do you think about when you're out digging?"

He thought for a minute. "What the spot was like hundreds of years ago. Who lived there . . . what they were like." He hesitated. "Sometimes I wonder if they had the same feelings that we do."

No one had ever expressed such feelings to Tessa Mae. She pressed on. "Do your mother and father understand your thinking like that?"

He smiled. "Not really. My father's a lawyer in Philadelphia. He didn't want me to come down here to school. He wanted me to be a doctor. My mother died when I was born. I think about her sometimes. I wished she could have lived and had lots of brothers and sisters for me to play with." The smile slipped away. "My father was busy, and I was alone most of the time with housekeepers. He's never gotten married again."

"I don't think she would want you to feel so sad," Tessa Mae said softly. She wanted to reach out and touch Guy's arm, but she couldn't.

Guy poked at the fire with his stick. It was dying down to coals that glowed red. "I know she wouldn't, but I do."

Suddenly he sat up straighter and grinned at Tessa Mae. "Enough about me. Do you have any brothers or sisters?"

"No, but I have a friend with a big family. I'll take you to meet them sometimes if you like." After I'm sure they'd like you, she added to herself.

"That would be fine."

They got quiet again, but Tessa Mae didn't want to get up and go to bed, breaking the spell. She'd started to feel comfortable with Guy. Maybe it would be all right for him to be around all summer.

He looked at her. "How old are you?"

"How old are *you*?"

"I'm nineteen." He grinned and waited for her answer.

Tessa Mae hesitated. "I'm . . . fourteen," she finally said.

"You seem older. I never expected to find such a pretty girl down here in the woods. I hope we can be friends."

Tessa Mae felt her face start to heat up again. She didn't think a boy had ever told her she was pretty. And even if she knew she wasn't, she didn't mind his saying so. What if she answered that she never expected to find a boy down here with her daddy who looked like Van Johnson? Tessa Mae smiled to herself. Whoooeee, she thought. He sure would think I'm silly.

She hoped they could be friends, too, but she didn't say that either. Instead she said, "We'd better go to bed. The birds won't let us sleep past dawn. And Roy Glen likes to get an early start."

Earlier in the evening, before dark, Tessa Mae had thrown her blanket onto a piece of ground that had no rocks or weeds. Now she rolled into it and tried to sleep. But she lay thinking for a long time, watching the sky fill up with stars before she could even shut her eyes.

A few things were starting to go right for her. Why not hope for more?

CHAPTER
SIXTEEN

Roy Glen had coffee made when Tessa Mae came awake to the harsh, *helio, helio, helio* of blue jays. In the distance floated the clear warble of a hermit thrush. The smell of the coffee mingled with the perfume of the rich, earthy, bottom-land soil. She couldn't help making a contrast to the concrete and dust smells in town, and the sounds of cars and people.

Grabbing a small flour sack she'd brought to hold her personal belongings, she rolled out of her blanket and slipped off to the river. Young willow trees clustered alongside maple and river birch, creating deep pools of shade. She savored the cool air of the morning as she flopped on the riverbank and placed her feet in the water. There was no need for her to hurry. Time had again become like the river, and as she dipped in and used a little, it would be replaced by more, easing by in a steady flow.

She dug in her sack and found her hair brush. Unbraiding her long hair, she brushed and wove it back together in the one cool, neat braid down her back. She washed carefully, then satisfied that she looked her best, she returned to camp.

Roy Glen poured her a cup of coffee. She tipped the tin of canned milk until the coffee was the muddy color she liked and stirred in a spoon of sugar.

Knowing Roy Glen seldom ate breakfast when he was alone, she didn't expect anything as grand as bacon frying or water bubbling for oatmeal. Still, she was hungry. "Where's the feller who said he'd fix breakfast?" She smiled at her daddy.

"I can have half this bottom land dug up before that boy wakes of a mornin'," Roy Glen said. "But he's smart. Catches on fast and sniffs out relics like an old hound dog. Those were fine spear points he found. Do you like him, honey?"

"He's okay. You 'spect—expect he'll last all summer?"

"I don't mind if he does. Long as he quits lecturin' me on givin' my finds to the museum."

"Promise me I can stay, too, Daddy."

"I don't mind if you do. It's fixin' to be as crowded as town down here though." Roy Glen smiled and sipped his coffee. "I've got to go to town this mornin'. You kids are eatin' up all the food."

"Will you see Mama?" Tessa Mae opened the wooden box where her father kept the bacon, eggs, and the opened tin of milk. The box had been pushed up under the exposed roots of a huge sycamore, largest of all Ozark trees. All around, the ground was damp from the trickle of a small stream. The shade and dampness kept the food almost as fresh as an icebox would.

The campground was backed up by a cliff and was partially set on a gravel bar. It was no place to be in time of flood, but cool and clear of undergrowth, near the river, so they had a constant water supply. Roy Glen had built the fire beside a huge log, weathered smooth and left there by a previous flood. Tessa Mae sat on the log beside her father and laid slabs of bacon across the skillet. If Guy was going to sleep until noon, she might as well start breakfast.

She repeated her question. "Are you going to see Mama, Roy Glen?"

"No reason to, and I don't 'spect she wants to see me. You want to come with me? You can go and visit yer mother if you like."

Just then, Guy came out of the woods. His hair was tousled and his face crinkled with leftover sleep. "You two were going to cut out and leave me here in the wilds alone, weren't you?"

"You asked for it, sleeping all day." Tessa Mae grinned at his early morning face, looking like a little kid's. "And all that talk about fixing breakfast was just talk. You want an egg?"

"Two." He grinned at her and yawned. "Coffee, black." He didn't say any more until he'd eaten a big plate of bacon and eggs and three pieces of bread and jelly.

"Roy Glen's going to town to get more food," Tessa Mae told Guy. "Looks like we may need it."

Guy laughed. "I'm a growing boy. I don't mean to eat all your food, though, Roy Glen. I'll buy some groceries. The one thing my father gives me plenty of is money, even if he doesn't approve of my being here."

"We're three outcasts on an island," Tessa Mae said. "Like in that movie where they found the treasure of diamonds."

"It's Saturday, Tessa Mae. We can see what's playing at the movie theater in Lamar. Want to?" Guy wiped out the skillet, leaving the bacon grease to coat it for cooking another meal. After they had eaten, he took their plates to the river again to scrub with sand. Now he seemed to be looking forward to going to town.

"I can see we're not going to get any work done today." Roy Glen rolled himself a cigarette, looking as if he were in no hurry to move.

"We'll work better tomorrow for having a day off, won't we, Tessa Mae?"

Having Guy here could actually be fun. Tessa Mae saw that he wasn't going to treat her like some kid who was in the way. The truth was that she'd love to see a movie— that was the only thing from town that she would miss.

"Okay, let's go get the truck. I don't aim to carry a ton of groceries two miles. I figure I can get it pretty close to here since the woods are dry." Roy Glen started walking towards home. Guy and Tessa Mae hurried to follow as soon as Guy had poured water on the fire and covered it with a couple of shovelsful of dirt.

When they drove into Lamar, the three of them squished in the front seat of the old Dodge, Roy Glen said, "Did you ever get them shorts, honey?" He pulled some money from his pocket, a big roll of money, and peeled off a ten-dollar bill. "Get yourself a hat, too. It'll be mighty hot before long."

She stared at the roll of money, wishing her mama could see it. Then, incredulously, she took the ten-dollar bill.

"It's all yours," Roy Glen said, grinning. "Now, go on while I go to the post office. I'll meet you at the grocery store."

Tessa Mae had never had ten dollars to spend on herself at one time. She was glad when Guy said he had some errands and left her on her own. At Repan's Department

Store, she considered almost everything in her size before she chose two pairs of shorts, two sleeveless blouses, a straw hat with a big brim, and two bandanna scarves. Adding the total in her head, she figured it was about seven dollars and fifty cents. Then after a moment's hesitation, she stopped at the lingerie department and looked at some brassieres. But when she glanced up at the checkout counter, she saw the clerk watching her. Quickly, she dropped the brassieres and walked towards the register, chin high. She paid the total and hugged the sack to her, feeling richer than Erline Crider and Sue Anne Sparks put together.

At Miller's grocery she got a Pepsi-Cola and an ice cream cup. A movie magazine caught her eye while she waited, but she figured it would be out of place to read it while they were camping in the woods. Instead, she bought a spiral notebook and two pencils. She'd start a new book, a journal like Thoreau's. In it she'd write down the name and behavior of all the animals and birds she saw. She'd note what was growing near their camp, and every night, she promised herself, she'd put in her thoughts about the day. She laughed at the notion that some day students would have to read her journal and explain what they thought she meant.

Sitting on the curb outside the grocery, waiting for Roy Glen or Guy to come along, Tessa Mae considered visiting her mama, or Elbert and Maudie. She'd told Maudie she was going to live with Roy Glen all summer, but she hadn't said good-bye before she left. Licking the ice cream cup lid, she told herself it was okay not to visit anyone today. Jane Wyman smiled back at her from the lid as if to say that it was the right decision and she shouldn't feel guilty about it.

She had eaten half her ice cream when she heard someone

whisper, "Hey, Tessa Mae. It's me, Jec. I thought you was goin' to go live in the woods with your daddy."

Tessa Mae looked around. Jec was leaning on the brick wall of the grocery store, in the alley, but close enough to talk to her.

"Don't turn around! I'm waitin' for it to be time for the movie to start. You goin'? If you are I kin sneak away and come find you in the woods tomorrow. We kin talk about it." It sounded to Tessa Mae as if Jec had minded his mother about as long as was natural for him.

"We're campin' down off a sandbar where the river gets wider, Jec," Tessa Mae said, as if she was talking to herself. "Come on down." She figured no one would see them together that deep in the woods. She wanted to tell Jec about Guy. That way if they ever met, Jec wouldn't be surprised at her having a new friend. She was used to telling Jec everything, and it seemed natural to keep doing so even though she was having a different kind of summer.

"My sister Florella liked to died havin' that ole baby," Jec whispered. "It was too little, though, and it didn't live. Would have been a boy."

"Jec! You mean it?" Tessa Mae stood up, forgetting she wasn't supposed to be talking to him. "Is Florella all right? Is she still goin' to get married?"

"I reckon. We was all powerful scared." Jec stood, leaning on the wall, hands in his pockets, looking at his bare feet. He was still pretending not to be talking to Tessa Mae. "Well, I reckon I'd better go on down to the movie theater, Tessa Mae. My friend Russell's goin' to meet me there. I'll see you."

"Not if I—" Tessa Mae started to say, "see you first," but a voice cut her off.

"Lookee here, Dusty. It's Tessa Mae. I never knowed

you was a nigger lover as well as strange, Tessa Mae." It was Chester Wilcox and two of the other big boys from eighth grade.

"Run, Jec," Tessa Mae whispered as the boys approached her.

Jec's eyes got huge and he glanced around. There was no use running back into the alley. The space beside the stores was a dead end, where delivery trucks backed in and unloaded. Chester Wilcox, Dusty McGuire, and Jimmy Joe Hardy blocked Jec's way to the street.

"I think we'd better teach this little black boy a lesson, don't you, Jimmy Joe?" Chester said. He started walking towards Jec, who backed up slowly. "It ain't nice to talk to white girls, even if that white girl is trash like Tessa Mae Ferris. Don't you know that, black boy?"

"You shut your mouth, Chester Wilcox," Tessa Mae said in her fanciest tone. "It's none of your business who I talk to. Might be some colored boys in this town fourteen times more interesting than you and your friends here." Tessa Mae had spoken without thinking and now she had just made things worse.

Chester laughed. "I can't help it if you don't know who to be seen with, Tessa Mae, but we can sure make this black boy remember his place."

With all her strength, Tessa Mae flew at Chester, arms flailing. "Run, Jec, run," she screamed. "Get outta here."

Chester threw up his arms to protect himself. Then he grabbed one of Tessa Mae's wrists. They scuffled for a second. Chester got hold of both her arms, throwing her off balance and knocking her down on the gravel in the alleyway.

Pain shot up one arm and her leg as she hit the sharp

stones. But she sat up immediately, frantic about Jec. Jimmy Joe and Dusty had taken off after him when he dashed past her, and now Chester was joining the chase.

There was nothing she could do. It was up to Jec to escape. Looking at her scraped knee and elbow, she held back tears. When was she ever going to learn some sense? She should have known it wasn't safe to talk to Jec in the middle of town. Now Jec was running for his life, or he would get beaten up, and she was bleeding from the spill she'd taken.

Guy and Roy Glen had come out of the post office in time to see the last of the confrontation. "Tessa Mae, what happened?" Guy rushed up to her and crouched beside her. "Are you all right?"

"You're too big to be fightin', Tessa Mae." Roy Glen cut off Guy's concern. " 'Pears I raised me a wildcat instead of a lady." He sounded more disgusted than worried about Tessa Mae.

"They were goin' to hurt Jec," she said sharply. "I wasn't thinkin'. I got Jec in trouble. If they catch him, they'll beat him up." Tessa Mae got up slowly. Guy reached out to help her. Her knee had gotten stiff and pain shot up and down her leg.

"If you're talking about that black boy, he was a block ahead of three boys who were after him. I don't think you need to worry." Guy helped Tessa Mae put her weight on her knee.

Tessa Mae was worried. She'd got Jec in trouble, just like Bertha had predicted. It didn't matter that Jec had started talking first. She was older than Jec. She should have reminded him of their promise to Bertha.

Roy Glen had gone on into Miller's grocery, the frown still on his face. As she followed him inside, Tessa Mae acknowledged that although he seldom scolded her, she really deserved it this time.

Tessa Mae went into the bathroom at the grocery and cleaned up her scrapes, pressing on the skinned places to stop the bleeding. When she went back out, she was trying not to limp, but her leg still stung. She looked around for Roy Glen and Guy, not really wanting to see Guy now that she'd made a complete fool of herself.

Roy Glen was putting a carton of cigarettes into the pile of supplies he'd loaded into a cart. Tessa Mae stopped beside him.

"I'm sorry for actin' like such a fool, Roy Glen. I'm findin' it right hard to become a lady overnight. See, I'm even finding it hard to talk like one. Think you could forgive me?"

Roy Glen kept staring at the display of Camel cigarettes. "I'd think you'd know better than to be fighting on the street like that at your age."

"I do know better, Roy Glen. Something came over me so quick I just forgot. I promise I'll work on the problem."

"Well, I reckon I could overlook it this time, Tessa Mae, if you don't think it'll happen again."

"I'm sure it won't." The weight that had settled on Tessa Mae's shoulders lifted. It was in Roy Glen's nature to forgive easily, but she always found it hard to apologize.

"Get yerself some of that Spearmint gum you favor, you hear," Roy Glen said, the gesture reinforcing his forgiveness. "And some candy bars."

Tessa Mae finished pushing the cart into the checkout stand while Roy Glen prepared to pay. She looked around to find Guy behind her.

Guy had cans of peanuts, candy bars, a *Life* magazine, and two notebooks topping off his load of purchases. Maybe she wasn't the only one who was going to keep a journal like Thoreau. "Dear Diary," she imagined him writing. "Today I met this wonderful girl who likes sleeping on the ground and digging Indian relics. Now we're going to the movies together, or we were until she got into a fight with three boys and got all skinned up. I had hoped she could be my girl friend, but now I know she's too young."

Guy turned to Tessa Mae as they carried the boxes of groceries towards the truck. "Now we can go to the movie. Still want to?"

"I'd like that," she said quietly.

"I reckon we'd better eat some lunch in the cafe," Roy Glen said. "Then I'll go to the house and look over the mail and you two can go to the movies."

The food in the cafe looked better than it had when she and her mother ate there. Tessa Mae ordered roast beef with brown gravy smothering the meat, bread and potatoes, but after she ate a couple of bites the food stuck in her throat. She couldn't help worrying about Jec.

"You think I got Jec in a heap of trouble, Roy Glen?" she asked. "I knew I shouldn't have been talking to him, but I forgot."

"Knowin' Jec, Tessa Mae," Roy Glen replied. "I figure he can take care of himself. I think you'd best forget it."

Guy looked at Roy Glen and then Tessa Mae. Maybe he wanted to ask some questions, but he didn't. Instead he groaned and said, "I didn't leave room for popcorn. Aren't you going to eat more than that, Tessa Mae?"

Tessa Mae looked into his blue eyes that kept smiling at her after his mouth had stopped. "I guess the heat in town has made me lose my appetite."

Tessa Mae knew there was a much better reason than the heat for her being unable to eat. She'd never been to the movies with a boy before. She longed to suggest that they go back to camp, but Guy would never understand why she'd changed her mind. And she couldn't tell him the reason, that she'd got a bad case of nerves. Everything that was happening today made her feel like a child, reminding her she was only fourteen and Guy was five years older.

Before she could change her mind, Roy Glen took off for home, leaving her standing there with Guy. She'd have to get through the rest of the day the best she could. When they crossed Main Street, she saw Chester, Jimmy Joe, and Dusty walking towards the theater. They must have given up on catching Jec. That made her feel better right away.

As they were waiting in line in front of the Lamar Grand, Guy casually put one arm around Tessa Mae. With the other, he cradled his stomach. "I'm stuffed," he said, "but wait till you taste my cooking. You'll sneak right back in here to the cafe."

"Can't be worse than Roy Glen's," she said and began to relax with him again. Guy was so easy to be with, just like Jec in a way. The Grand was showing *The Road to Utopia*, Bob Hope and Bing Crosby's newest *Road* movie. She and Guy were rerunning the plot of their last movie when Tessa Mae noticed a group of girls looking their way.

It was Erline Crider's crowd, all of them dressed in tight shorts. Sue Anne Sparks had an especially big grin on her face. Sue Anne's hair was as thin as a frog's, and she wore wire glasses, but Tessa Mae knew she thought she was special. They were whispering and all but pointing to Guy. Satisfaction made Tessa Mae forget everything for a few minutes: the pain in her arm and knee, even Chester's chasing after Jec. She figured that none of those girls had gone on a real date before, and here she was getting ahead of them—dumb, backward Tessa Mae. She looked right at Erline, smiled and waved, just like they were best of friends.

But when she turned and realized the line was moving, she spotted Russell Lewis, Jec's other best friend. He was standing beside the theater, waiting for Jec. Tessa Mae couldn't holler and tell Russell what happened. She couldn't even acknowledge that she'd seen him if he looked her way. The misery flooded back, worse than ever. She had spoiled Jec's pleasure in the movie, too. Once he'd gotten away from Chester, he wouldn't dare to come back. The little bit of lunch she'd eaten squirmed in her stomach.

"Want some popcorn?" Guy asked when they got inside. The buttery smell and crackling noise of popping corn caught their attention as it was supposed to do.

She shook her head no and waited until Guy got some. "Bet you end up eating half of mine," he teased.

"I'm not very hungry."

"Are you all right? Does your arm hurt?"

She couldn't tell him that what hurt was being the cause of Jec's missing a movie for the first time in his life. She just shook her head and tried to smile.

The Lamar Grand may have been the only movie theater in town but it was truly grand. J. H. Hamilton, who owned the peach orchard and half of Lamar, had bought it two years ago and redecorated it with unheard-of opulence in the style of a certain theater in Memphis. The local newspaper had written a big article about the opening that showed a picture of Mr. Hamilton cutting a red ribbon stretched across the theater's gold-painted doors. Another photo had him wearing a funny hat and scooping up fresh popcorn from a fancy new machine.

Tessa Mae would never forget her first visit after the opening. Even now as the lights dimmed and the thick, heavy red velvet curtains drew up in scallops, she realized she was holding her breath. Then the tiny stars on the ceiling began to glow. As always, she tried to see how many she could count before the previews started. Jec told her there were three hundred, but she figured he was guessing. He'd never missed a minute of the movie to count them all either.

Guy didn't say a word during the previews, but she hoped he'd want to come back every Saturday. Tessa Mae hated to skip a movie. Those darkened Saturday afternoons were the highlight of her week. Next was a Woody Woodpecker cartoon and Guy laughed as much as she did.

They had sat down near the front as Tessa Mae always did, and as always, when the serial came on, Tessa Mae shuddered. It was chapter eight of *Captain America* titled "Cremation in the Clouds." For weeks the crime-fighting district attorney, Grant Gardner, in his secret identity of Captain America, had been battling the sinister Scarab. The Scarab was really Dr. Maldor, curator of the Drummond Museum, who was bitter because other people had claimed discoveries he'd made on an archaeological expedition years before.

Last week's episode closed with Captain America inside the Tec-Ni-Gas Oil Company when it exploded, and Tessa Mae was relieved to see that he'd escaped from the building just in time. "Isn't she beautiful?" whispered Tessa Mae, as Gail Richards came on the screen. She was Gardner's girl friend. "Oh, no, she doesn't know the Scarab had a bomb put in her plane."

Gail got ready to fly her airplane and finally started the engine. The bomb mechanism was rigged to the motor and as soon as she started it, the bomb began to tick. One–two–three. Tessa Mae hunched down in her seat. The suspense was terrible. There was a huge explosion on the screen and the picture faded out.

"Aughhhh," everyone in the theater shouted.

Guy laughed. "I suppose you'll just *have* to come back next week to see if she got out."

"I always do." Tessa Mae and Guy laughed and she realized it was fun to share the movie instead of seeing it alone, which was her usual way. They shared whispered comments during the main feature, too, and it was over much too soon. Tessa Mae promised herself she'd find Jec and tell him all about the movie and especially the serial. He hated missing the serial most of all.

The bright sun surprised her as it always did when she came out of the dark, cool theater, back to real life. Roy Glen had said he'd pick them up about four o'clock. Tessa Mae hoped he wouldn't get busy and forget. He was as bad about forgetting the time when he was in his office as he was down by the river.

She and Guy sat on a rock wall outside the theater and replayed the story just as she and Jec would have done. That made her feel even worse about Jec's missing the movie.

"Well, lookee here, guys. It's Tessa Mae with another date. Ain't she become popular?" Chester and his sidekicks had found them. "Does he know your other sweetheart is a black boy?"

Tessa Mae felt the steam inside her rising, but she looked away as if she'd never heard what Chester said. Guy put his hand on her arm, and that helped her calm down. She sure didn't want to make a fool of herself again.

"Friend of yours?" Guy asked when Chester gave up on getting a response and started chasing Jimmy Joe and Dusty down the street.

"Hardly. Best to ignore him," she said. Still, when Roy Glen appeared in the battered Dodge truck, Tessa Mae waved gratefully. After today, the woods were going to seem more peaceful than ever. But before Tessa Mae and Guy could get up off the rock wall, who should pull up beside Roy Glen but Reverand Peterson and Mama.

CHAPTER
S E V E N T E E N

Tessa Mae straightened her shoulders and stood up.

"Now what's wrong?" Guy asked.

"You stay here, Guy. This is family." Tessa Mae walked over to where Roy Glen was sitting in the Dodge. Reverend Peterson and her mother got out of the car. The Reverend Peterson had on his let's-be-Christian-about-this face.

"Roy Glen," her mother started the conversation. "Dixie Lee called me this afternoon and told me she saw Tessa Mae going off to the movie with a boy. I figured I could find her here. I never agreed to let Tessa Mae live with you down there in the woods all summer. She took off while I was at work. I had guessed where she was, but I hadn't had time to come lookin' fer her."

"You did too agree, Mama," Tessa Mae said. "You said, 'go off and live down there. I don't care.'"

"I said that when I was mad and you know it." Her mother turned back to Roy Glen. "My lawyer says Tessa Mae should be stayin' with me until the divorce is final, and then he's sure I'll get legal custody of her anyway."

"Judge Noble said I could stay all summer with my daddy."

"Only if we both agreed, and that was just an opinion, not anything legal. My lawyer called that judge. You twisted his words to suit yer plans, young lady, and I don't agree to what yer up to."

"Daddy, you tell her. Tell her you agreed for me to stay with you. Tell her it's all right." Tessa Mae tightened her fists, but she was beginning to feel helpless again. It seemed as if no amount of fighting or words was going to convince her mother.

" 'Pears to me as how there ain't no harm in it, Vinnie." Roy Glen spoke from the safety of the truck. "She's some help to me and she likes the work. I can pay her if that's your problem."

"She can get a decent job in town. And there is so harm in it, too. It's all over town about how that college boy is livin' with you down there in the woods, gittin' mail like he plans to stay all summer. It won't take two days before the talk will switch to Tessa Mae bein' down there with you, sleepin' out with you two men."

Tessa Mae could see that the fact that one of the two men was her daddy didn't swing any weight with Mama.

"I'll get the sheriff if I need to, Roy Glen. You know I will." Tessa Mae's mother stood with her hands on her hips. She wasn't going to run off crying this time. She had on her I-mean-business look, and Tessa Mae started to get scared although being afraid wouldn't help her any.

"I know you can get the sheriff, Vinnie," Roy Glen said. "And the preacher—the whole town. All the help you need on your side. But I'm lookin' after Tessa Mae good. She's not goin' to get in any trouble."

"I know how you'll look after her, Roy Glen—just like you look after yerself and yer business. She'll do as she pleases and you'll not say a word to her."

"I'll run away, Mama," Tessa Mae said, fear giving force to her threat. "You have the sheriff bring me back to town, and I'll leave while you're at work. You'll have to tie me up and lock me in to keep me in that little old house, or else you'll have to put me in jail. Lamar must be havin' a bunch of fun now, talkin' about this. What'll they have to say if you have to put yer daughter in jail to keep her from running off?"

Mama was being put to a real test. She would have to decide if she wanted her way enough not to worry about what people thought. She stared at her daughter until Tessa Mae had to look away. She turned to Roy Glen and made her eyes say, help me. For once in your life, stand up to Mama and help me out.

"I reckon she's as stubborn and strong-minded as you are, Vinnie," Roy Glen said, holding back a grin.

"Tell them, Reverend Peterson. Tell them that Tessa Mae livin' down there with two men is a sin." Tessa Mae's mother was starting to look flustered.

"Well now, Vinnie," the Reverend Peterson said slowly. "Tessa Mae's just being down there working with Roy Glen is no sin. He is her daddy. While it don't look too good and may ruin Tessa Mae's reputation some, the situation itself is within the law. Unless you want to get a court order to make Tessa Mae stay with you. Then you'll have to enforce it or have the sheriff help you."

Tessa Mae could see her mother pondering on which was the worse of two evils.

"It's just for the summer, Mama," Tessa Mae begged.

Her mother sighed, and finally said, "Well, it's against my good judgment, Tessa Mae. But if you're goin' to be so headstrong about it, and Roy Glen promises to keep you out of trouble—"

"Oh, Mama, I'll stay out of trouble. I promise I will." Tessa Mae wanted to hug her mother, but she didn't. "And I'll come to see you the next time we're in town. I'll come over to the laundry if you're not home."

Reverend Peterson held the door as her mother got back into the car. "I'll pray for you, Tessa Mae," he said, "to help you to see the misery you're causing your mother. To end up doing what's right for you and her both."

"You do that, Reverend Peterson," Tessa Mae said.

Mama had her head turned away from Tessa Mae when they pulled out, and without wanting to, Tessa Mae felt a wave of sadness wash over her. Her mother was most likely crying. While she was so afraid, Tessa Mae hadn't been able to think about how her mother might feel. Now she just didn't want to. Mama might want her in town badly, but Tessa Mae wanted something different. She wanted to go with Roy Glen.

Trying to forget everything but the future, she slid into the front seat of the truck alongside Roy Glen. Roy Glen honked at Guy, who had started walking down the street and Tessa Mae moved over to make room as he opened the door and jumped in.

She didn't look at him as she said, "Everything's all right now. We're set for the summer. I'm going to work really hard, Roy Glen, I promise. I'm going to find something special. We'll have a real good time down there by the river this summer. You won't be sorry I'm there."

Roy Glen didn't speak, nor did Guy, but when Tessa Mae

glanced at Guy he was looking at her, smiling. Roy Glen turned the truck around and they drove through Lamar past the Lamar Grand, Miller's grocery, and the post office. Tessa Mae knew she wouldn't be coming back to town, not for a good long time.

As wooded areas replaced stores and houses, as the cool green of the road to the camp closed around them, Tessa Mae imagined that the road was a tunnel. On one side of the tunnel, the side they were leaving, was the prison called Lamar. A small-town prison where people gossiped about other people's business, where kids made fun of her because she wasn't like them. On the other side, in the dim shadows of late evening, was freedom, a freedom she had tasted and relished and now craved. Life in town was a story she had read over and over, a school book that was predictable and suffocating.

The summer ahead was not yet written, but promised adventure and surprise. Tessa Mae leaned back between her two friends, one old, one new, and closed her eyes. She no longer felt anxious or rushed. The surprises would find her as the summer unfolded.

CHAPTER
EIGHTEEN

Early the next morning, as soon as breakfast was over and the camp neatened up, Tessa Mae told Roy Glen she had some unfinished business and took off for Jec's. There wasn't any way she could enjoy any of the summer unless she stopped feeling guilty over what had happened in town. As she neared the Browns' yard, she heard Rose Ann singing, then spotted her pushing Lilly Belle in an old tire swing that hung from a limb of the oak tree. Dee-Dee sat close by in the dirt running a toy truck round and round a make-believe town.

"Howdy, Rose Ann," Tessa Mae said. "You baby-sittin'?"

"Yes. Mama done gone to church."

"Is Jec here?"

"No, he gone off to church, too. We the only ones here."

"Can you play with us, Tessa Mae?" Dee-Dee asked. "I've got me a right nice town here."

"No, I have to get to work," said Tessa Mae, vexed with herself for not having come earlier. "Can you get me a pencil and a piece of paper, Rose Ann? I have to write Jec a note."

"What about?" Rose Ann asked.

"I want to tell him where we're campin', Miss Nosy," Tessa Mae teased. Rose Ann obviously didn't know anything about what had happened in town the day before. It figured that Jec wouldn't have told his mama, or any of the family. He'd have risked Bertha saying he couldn't go to town at all. Tessa Mae pushed Lilly Belle while Rose Ann went into the house.

She returned with a piece of tablet paper and a stub of a pencil. On the back of the paper was one of Jec's school lessons with an *A* at the top. "Good work," the teacher had added in her red pencil.

Tessa Mae sat down on the step to write.

> *Dear Jec,*
> *I'm truly sorry about what happened yester-*
> *day, and especially that you missed the movie.*
> *I'll tell you all about it the next time I see you.*
> *We're camping down on the river by Mr.*
> *Klauber's fields. Come on down and see us.*
>
> *Your friend,*
> *Tessa Mae*

"Will you see that Jec gets this, Rose Ann?" Tessa Mae said, folding the paper over and over until it was a small square. "It's real important."

"Sure, Tessa Mae." Rose Ann was sitting in the tire swing, Lilly Belle in her lap, twisting it round and round, then letting it spin. She stopped, took the note, and put it in the pocket of her dress. Dee-Dee grabbed the pencil and ran off to the house. "Want to swing?" she called.

"No, I have to go. See you when I see you." Tessa Mae

waved and took off down the trail. She felt better. When Jec showed up at their camp, they could talk it all out. Then their friendship would be back to normal.

She had no trouble finding Roy Glen and Guy, who had climbed to where Guy had found the two spear points. The texture of the earth indicated that over the years the river had widened its course, then receded again, leaving the ground sandy. Most of the bottom land was rich farm country because of the river's occasional flooding.

The fields to the east of them belonged to a farmer named Henry Klauber who had unearthed some Indian relics during spring plowing. Roy Glen had emptied several graves on land that now was filled with neat rows of growing corn.

"I figure these two points you found, Guy, were washed out of the field above us," Roy Glen said, tugging at his old felt hat. Then he pointed. "See that there gully? It starts up the other side of this field and comes right down to where we're standin'. Where one grave is, there's likely to be several. When the river floods or when we have a gully-washer of a rain storm like we did in early May, pieces from the old graves will wash out."

"You said you found some graves, Roy Glen," Guy said. "Wouldn't the farmer have plowed over all the rest that are up there by now?"

"Not necessarily. Depends on how recent the grave, how many times the river has flooded and covered this land with silt. There may be even more graves up there deep in the ground."

"Couldn't there have been only one grave if someone died while they were traveling?" Tessa Mae was pleased to show her knowledge. She knew that Indians in this area moved with the game, the trading possibilities, or to visit other tribes. She felt so proud, standing there by Roy Glen as if he were a real teacher and she and Guy were students.

"Yes, but there were permanent camps all along this river. As permanent as an Indian camp could be. Take that spot where we're campin'. Indians may have stayed there for the same reason we're favorin' it. It's far enough from the river not to have changed much. There's more trees today, bigger ones, but the shelter of the cliff overhangin' makes it a right good place to settle in for a spell." Roy Glen pulled the pack of Camels from his pocket and lit up. While the cigarette dangled between his lips, he squatted and sifted through the dirt at the end of the gully with Guy kneeling beside him.

Tessa Mae stood watching them, daydreaming, then walked away, leaving the two men poking around in the sand and rocks. It was hard for her to think while she was with Guy. Instead of keeping her eyes open for a rock with an unusual shape, or a chip of pottery that might give her a clue as to where to dig, she found herself watching him.

Tessa Mae never heard from Jec. But in the peace of the summer days, the unhappiness she had felt in May disappeared. June passed and a pattern developed to their lives. By day they usually separated, poking around in likely-looking places, digging in shady banks, sifting dirt and rocks for clues. More often Guy hunted with Roy Glen, but Tessa Mae wandered as free as the woods creatures did now that food was plentiful. It was enough for her to be with her father at night, listening to him talk, teaching Guy what he knew. She learned, too, and then put the knowledge to work by day.

Often Guy followed the gully eastward through Klauber's fields, the corn growing tall on either side of him. Occasionally Tessa Mae went with him, and she enjoyed his company. She hadn't planned to get all silly over boys, and she wasn't silly now, but she did like his smile when he'd catch her eye, his excitement if he thought he'd found something. She liked talking to him, or more often, listening, because he'd been so many places. He'd tell stories about visiting the Indian mounds at Spiro, Oklahoma, or the museums in Philadelphia and New York. He made her want to go to those places, too.

Roy Glen spent several days digging in a pile of shells downstream from their camp, yet still near the river. He said he figured it was where the Indians had harvested fresh-water mussels, opening and leaving the shells. Over the years much of the pile had undoubtedly been washed away, but there was always the possibility that it had been used for a dump, too. Near the bottom he turned up a couple of scrapers. Someone had broken them, perhaps while removing hair from a deer hide before it was softened into material for clothes or shoes.

One afternoon Roy Glen and Guy went off together to climb up to a cave that Roy Glen said he hadn't explored. Since Tessa Mae didn't like caves, she decided to hike back to the house. Bundling up her dirty clothes, she set off, comfortable on the familiar trail. She hesitated at the turn-off to the Browns but then continued on home.

Roy Glen had locked the house up, but Tessa Mae knew where he'd hidden the key, and she let herself in, noticing the musty smell right away. The house seemed a place that no one cared about anymore. A floorboard creaked underfoot. She looked up, half expecting her mother to pop out of the kitchen and say, "It's about time you came back and cleaned up, Tessa Mae. Yer startin' to look and smell just like those dusty ghosts yer chasing after."

A longing to see her mother engulfed her and she was tempted to go into town. Instead she threw open all the windows and put water on the stove to heat.

She brought in the big galvanized tub from the garage and filled it part way with cold water from the well, then poured in the boiling water until it was just the right temperature. While the water was heating, she'd washed her clothes and hung them outside, hoping they'd be dry by the time she wanted them.

She sat soaking in the tub, letting her mind go free. Then she washed her hair and sat in the sun, wrapped in two old towels while her clothes swayed in the slight breeze.

Feeling a hundred percent better, she got dressed and headed back to camp. Once on the trail, though, she let her feet take her another way, towards Jec's.

She hadn't been there for weeks. It looked the same except for more weeds and bigger flowers at the front of the house. The garden was lush and must have been producing well. Rose Ann sat on the porch playing jacks.

"Howdy, Rose Ann," Tessa Mae said. "Jec around here anyplace?"

"Howdy, Tessa Mae. I don't know where Jec is. How come you don't come over anymore?"

"I'm workin' in the woods, way past your house, nearly two miles."

"You choppin' wood?" Rose Ann bounced the ball and picked up all the jacks at once, patting the floor at the same time.

Tessa Mae laughed. "No, I'm diggin' for Indian relics."

Rose Ann started spreading the jacks for the next game, ignoring Tessa Mae as she concentrated on picking up one at a time. *Bonk, bonk,* the ball bounced on the weathered wooden floor of the porch.

Tessa Mae had an impulse to join the game. She was about to sit down when Jec came out of the house.

"Whoooeee, Lordy, Jec, you've got taller." Tessa Mae

stared at him, amazed. Jec was almost as tall as she was.

Jec looked at Tessa Mae, then his mouth spread into a slow grin. "I reckon you ain't the only one growin' lately. Where you been? My mama sent me lookin' for you once to invite you to supper."

"Didn't you get my note? I told you we were down by the sand bars east of old man Klauber's fields." Tessa Mae looked at Rose Ann. She was singing softly now and still playing jacks. She hadn't given Jec the note, but Tessa Mae knew it wouldn't do any good to fuss at her over it.

"What note?" asked Jec.

"Never mind. Jec, I'm sorry about that time in town. I was sure worried that those boys would beat you up. And I'm sorry you missed the movie."

"That's okay. It was my fault, too." Jec jumped off the porch, then got quiet as he studied his toes. "I figured you'd stop by here more often since you didn't have to live with your mama in town."

"We've been busy. A student from the university is helping us this summer."

"A white boy?" Jec twisted his foot, drawing in the dirt with his big toe.

"Now, Jec, you know there aren't any black boys at the university." Tessa Mae laughed, thinking Jec was joking. She sat on the steps, hoping Jec would sit beside her.

"So you got better company than me?" Jec caught Rose Ann's ball when it bounced off the porch. He tossed it to her, all the while avoiding looking at Tessa Mae.

"Course not, Jec. But I have to work. You're workin' part time. My daddy's payin' me now. I'm savin' it for when I might want to go off to school. How's your job?" Tessa Mae realized that Jec was jealous of her spending time with someone else this summer. Remembering last year when they had fished almost every day, she knew things had changed for both of them—more things than getting taller.

"I reckon my job is okay. I didn't know you was workin', like at a real job, but my mama said you'd probably stop comin' around." Picking up a clod of dirt, Jec sent it flying towards a pecan tree. When it hit the trunk it broke up and scattered. A rusty red hen squawked and skittered away.

"Jec, that's not true," Tessa Mae said, dismayed. "I don't want to stop bein' friends. I jist got busy."

"Yeah, well maybe I'm busy, too." Jec ran up the steps past her and went into the house.

"You mad at Jec?" Rose Ann gathered her jacks and looked up at Tessa Mae.

"Of course not." Tessa Mae bit her lip.

"He mad at you?"

"I reckon he is." Tessa Mae sat back down on the porch steps, feeling empty and sad.

"Well, I'd better go in," said Rose Ann abruptly, disappearing into the house.

Tessa Mae looked up and saw the reason Rose Ann had left so suddenly. Bertha was hurrying down the trail. Tessa Mae smiled to herself. She'd bet Rose Ann was supposed to have done some chores before her mother got home.

"Howdy, Bertha," Tessa Mae said. Bertha looked hot, her dress dark with perspiration. Tessa Mae hadn't realized it was late enough for Bertha to be coming home.

"Howdy, Tessa Mae," Bertha said. "You been as scarce as hen's teeth."

"I reckon I have. You got plenty of work?" Tessa Mae moved away from the steps so Bertha could sit down.

"I surely do, child. Almost more than I can handle. Cuts into my fishin' time somethin' awful. When you comin' to supper? You and Roy Glen?"

"Soon I hope, Bertha. We get tired of camp cookin'."

"Just send me word in time to put in some extra potatoes. Jec's eatin' up all the extras lately." Bertha fanned herself with her pocketbook.

"He's growed up some." Tessa Mae wadded her hands into the top of the paper bag of clothes she carried.

"I guess he's goin' to get tall like his daddy and Everet. It happens all of a sudden sometimes."

"I think he's real mad at me."

"He's mopin' around some this summer, Tessa Mae, but it cain't be helped," Bertha said. "Even if your folks had stayed together, and you was livin' close by, it would have happened. I'm tryin' not to worry about him. Time will take care of the way he's feelin'."

"He thinks I don't care, Bertha. He ran away before I could tell him. Will you tell him I miss him, Bertha, that I really do care how he's feelin'?"

Bertha looked up at Tessa Mae, but she didn't smile. "I'll tell him, girl. I know you care. You visitin' your mama in town regular?" Bertha's question held a scolding tone.

"Are you tryin' to tell me somethin', Bertha? You tryin' to say that all I'm doin' is wrong? That I'm bein' selfish, thinkin' only of myself?" Tessa Mae stopped, startled by her own vehemence.

"I never said no such thing, but if you're thinkin' it, might be some truth in it."

"Nobody was thinkin' about me when all this misery happened," Tessa Mae said. "So I guess I have some right to take care of myself, seein' nobody else cares." Tessa Mae didn't want to break out crying in front of Bertha, but getting angry had turned loose a lot of feelings she had been collecting all day.

"There's a right smart lot of truth in that, too, Tessa Mae," Bertha said. "I reckon there's some things that happens that's like tossin' a rock in the middle of a fishin' pond. Little ripples washes out farther and farther till a lot of people get touched by the waves. Cain't nothin' be done to stop it, so we all have to live through it. Only time can smooth the pond back over."

Tessa Mae wondered if the pond she was thrashing around in would ever get smoothed over. The fact that Bertha cared enough to take time to talk to her helped some. "How's Florella, Bertha?"

"Well, 'pears she's mighty happy with Abe Pokewith. We all miss her somethin' awful, but I guess I done the right thing, lettin' her go." Bertha pushed her body upright, letting out a big sigh. "Should never have sat down till supper was cooked. You got time to stay and eat?"

"No, Bertha. I got to get goin'. It's my turn to cook."

"You mean some nights you eat yer daddy's cookin'?" Bertha laughed. "It's a wonder you haven't got so skinny you'd blow away."

"It's Guy's cookin' that's so bad. I got a new friend, Bertha," Tessa Mae said. "You'd like him. You said me and Roy Glen could come and eat sometime. Can I bring Guy, too?"

"He that growed-up boy from back East?" Bertha appeared to be thinking it over.

"It'd be all right, Bertha. I know him. I know it would."

"Well, if you say so, Tessa Mae, I reckon it'd be all right."

"It will be, Bertha. I've told him all about you and your family. We'll come real soon."

Bertha nodded and disappeared into the dim interior of the house while Tessa Mae set off down the trail to the camp.

CHAPTER
NINETEEN

Being isolated in the woods helped Tessa Mae forget the rest of the world. True to her resolve, she didn't go back to town when Roy Glen went for supplies. She pretended no one else existed except the three of them, and for a while it worked.

The summer was a time of wonderful freedom. She spent hours fishing or dozing beside the river. The robins nested where she could climb up and peek at their squeaking chicks, bills open, believing that Tessa Mae was their mother coming with worms. As quietly as ferns unfolding, the deer led their new fawns past her to drink from the river's edge. One evening when she fished until almost dusk, a raccoon family filed by, new bandits chittering as they rolled and fought and their mother dug into the soft ground for crayfish.

She filled her notebook with descriptions of how the year moved to high summer, each plant bursting into life in its time, each woods dweller going about its natural business.

And because she had a hunch that Indians *had* camped in their clearing, just as Roy Glen had said, she did most of her exploring nearby. One morning she was about half a mile from camp when a dark shape darted in front of her and disappeared into a hole in the bank of a dry creek bed. Head down, Tessa Mae was searching the rocky clutter for arrowheads or chert—the Ozark flint—when the shadowy form darted by.

Making herself comfortable, she sat, stone still, and waited to see what creature this was and what it was doing there. Her patience seemed to double in the woods, or perhaps it was that she had more patience with rocks and trees and animals and birds than she did with people. Many times she had kept silent for an hour, watching or waiting.

A mayfly with its long, threadlike body sailed past. A spider finished her web across the front of a ninebark bush. Often Tessa Mae had picked at the stem of the bush, trying to peel off nine successive layers, but she had never been successful.

From the opposite bank of the creek bed, about six feet from the hole, she saw the weasel clearly when it reappeared. The animal seemed young, and Tessa Mae guessed that it was female. Either she sensed no danger or her task was so all-consuming that she ignored the possible threat from Tessa Mae. Now half-hidden, the weasel resumed the excavation of her den, tossing dirt out behind her. Maybe that this was her first home and she didn't know that if it rained a lot the creek might fill and she would be washed out.

Twisting and turning, the slim, agile creature wiggled

and shaped the hole, kicking loose sand onto the stones in the creek with a *scritch, scratch*. Before she had dug very deep, however, something stopped her. She sniffed, peered inside, sniffed again, then shuffled off down the stream bed.

"Are you givin' it up?" Tessa Mae asked and giggled as the weasel fled her voice. "Can I see?"

She crossed the stream bed to examine the hole. That was when she found it: a broken slab of red pottery half hidden in the dirt. She picked it up and carefully brushed it off. A primitive pattern had been scraped into the red layer of mud that had been thinly spread over the pot's cream-colored surface and then left to harden. The design looked like part of the head and antlers of a deer.

She could feel excitement rising inside her like mercury in a thermometer on a July day. Practically running back to camp, staying with the stream bed until it met the narrow trail, she burst into the clearing. Neither Roy Glen nor Guy was anywhere to be seen but she didn't care. She had no intention of calling them just now. She grabbed a shovel and hurried back.

"Sorry if you planned to return, weasel," she said aloud as she carefully scooped sand and rock from the hole to enlarge it. Fortunately the ground was soft. As soon as the layer of sand was removed, the earth darkened and became rich with leaf mold. She gently slid her shovel in, lifting out only a cupful of dirt at a time. Then she felt it tap a solid object with a hollow thud.

The weasel had dug into the bank about a foot below the ground level, so now Tessa Mae started taking off the top layer, scraping more than digging with the shovel. Over and over she skinned the shovel carefully across the bank, inspecting the ground each time, looking for something besides dirt.

The air was hot and muggy, and she often stopped to wipe her face. Her blouse stuck to her shoulder blades, and loose dirt coated her arms and bare feet. But she kept on. Standing in the old stream bed, she scraped until the object she'd hit became visible.

It was a skull—a human skull. Tessa Mae had found a grave! She stepped back in fear and awe. Her hands started to shake. She dropped the shovel so that it clanked on the rocks. Sound reverberated all around her, followed by the silence that descends when a foreign sound invades the woods. Finally a fly rattled past her ear, setting her free of the spell.

Falling on her knees, Tessa Mae started to brush the crumbly black loam from the skull. Her hands moved quickly and skillfully, but her heart was filled with reverence. If this was an Indian grave—and what else could it be?—she had uncovered the body of a person who had lived here over a hundred years before.

The sun was halfway down the sky, filtering in through the leafy canopy of hickory nut leaves. A thrush, ignoring the afternoon heat, sang a cheerful song. Then again the forest dozed, waiting for the cool of evening. Tessa Mae sat beside the grave and stared at it, trying to conjure up the human being whose bones lay there. Pictures floated through her mind, but they were of Indians from the movies. Roy Glen said that real Indians weren't anything like them.

These people spent most of their lives gathering food and preserving it for the winter, enduring the cold, rainy seasons, then returning to the land again to support themselves. Their lives were simple, and she figured they were happy, as she would be happy if she could spend her whole life camped on the river, close to the earth.

There were things she would miss though, if she lived like those long-ago Indians, like reading and writing down her feelings and observations. And movies—she would really miss them. But if she'd never known about those things, maybe she'd find that sitting around a campfire, telling stories the way her daddy did, or picturing stories on pots and skins would be just as good.

Tessa Mae looked up to the sun, guessing it was about three o'clock. She didn't know enough about uncovering a grave to dig farther without risking damage to the contents. Now that she had gone this far, she would let her daddy and Guy help her. Besides—they deserved to share this excitement with her.

She covered the skull with a thin layer of earth. Then, leaning her shovel up over the front of the hole and lifting a leafy, dead tree branch carefully over the top, she set out to find Roy Glen. She wanted to tell him first. When she neared the camp she started to call out his name, then stopped. Somehow shouting didn't seem right to her in this quiet, wooded place. He wasn't in the camp, so she went on down the river about a quarter of a mile before spotting him slumped against a big chinquapin tree, his hat tilted over his face. Tessa Mae laughed. Roy Glen spent some of his digging time dozing, too.

But when she got close she knew he wasn't asleep. He smelled of liquor, and there was an empty whiskey bottle beside him.

"Daddy, Daddy, wake up. I have something to tell you." Tessa Mae tugged at his sleeve, but he only grumbled. "I found something. Something big and wonderful. You've got to come and see, help me with it."

Roy Glen mumbled something about being tired and not to bother him, then stretched out on the moss-covered ground. Tessa Mae couldn't get his attention again.

For a time she just sat watching his chest rise and fall. His face had gone slack. A short stubble of whiskers covered his chin. Saliva dribbled from the corner of his mouth, which hung slightly open.

Her mother's voice kept coming back to Tessa Mae. "Look at old man Groober. Go around him, Tessa Mae," her mother had said that morning in town. "What a disgrace. A sin. Someone should move him off the street."

How often did Roy Glen sleep off his drinking like this— passed out in the woods when Tessa Mae thought he was digging? Tears trickled down her face unbidden, unchecked. The call of a thrush, clear-toned and melodic, seemed out of place. Its song was so beautiful. How could the shy bird sing when her daddy lay sleeping off a drunk?

CHAPTER
TWENTY

After a few minutes Tessa Mae got up and slowly walked
back to the camp. Guy should be there soon. She'd get him
to help her move her daddy.

Out of habit she went to the river, rinsed the coffee pot,
and brought it back full of water. A few embers from the
fire site still glowed when she blew on them, so she broke
up tiny twigs to start the flames afresh.

Guy showed up at dusk with a big grin on his face.

"Don't say it." He stuck out his hand to stop her words.
"I know I'm late to dinner. But look what I brought you
from town." He reached into a double-layered brown bag
and brought out a Dixie cup of ice cream. "It's chocolate."

"Thanks, Guy, but—"

"I'm going to stand right here until you eat it. I drove
Roy Glen's truck like a madman to keep it cold."

His face was boyish again. She marveled at how he could look so serious until he smiled. She took the ice cream and pulled the tab, lifting the cardboard lid. It was June Allyson smiling up at her again, reminding her of Miss Criswell. The wedding must be soon. Tessa Mae licked chocolate from the lid. The ice cream had started to melt despite Guy's efforts but she liked it soft and creamy. Pushing all thoughts from her mind, she methodically ate the sweet, cool treat. At first it almost stopped at the lump in her throat, choking her. But then the lump eased, partly because Guy was being so kind.

Guy watched her, his blue eyes teasing.

"Where'd you go?" Tessa Mae had developed a style of eating from the Dixie cup, pulling the flat wooden spoon across her teeth without getting the taste of wood. She had a spoon in her mess kit, but it would have been cheating to use it.

"To Clarksville." He rummaged through the box of groceries and other supplies he had brought back. "I wanted to get my mail in Lamar, then I met a friend in Clarksville and forgot the time. I meant to get back by noon."

"A girl?" Tessa Mae felt she shouldn't have asked, but she was curious.

Guy's eyes were full of mischief. "Are you jealous?"

"Of course not. I was just curious. I'll bet you have a lot of girl friends. Why should I be jealous?" To her surprise, she was, just a little. She should have known Guy would have girl friends at his school.

"Most girls are, but since you have to know, it was a male friend, a friend who is jealous of me right now, and he doesn't even know I'm digging with anyone except Roy Glen. Hey, where is Roy Glen?"

Tessa Mae put her Dixie cup aside to wash. She might

want to store something in it later. Opening the coffee pot lid, she saw that the water was boiling and she dumped in six spoons of coffee. She might as well tell Guy the truth.

"He's drunk. Sleeping it off down there a piece." She nodded in the direction where she'd left Roy Glen. "I hoped you'd help me get him back here."

Guy frowned and poked at the fire with a stick. "He's too big for us to carry. Unless he can walk, we'll have to leave him there."

Tessa Mae knew he was right. "Then go with me to cover him up," she said, scooping up Roy Glen's blanket while Guy got a flashlight. They found their way along a makeshift path, perhaps a deer trail, to where Roy Glen slept on the ground.

"Daddy. Daddy, wake up." Tessa Mae tugged at his sleeve, but he barely moved. She spread the army blanket over him, tucking it under him as best she could.

Neither she nor Guy said anything going out or back. A big orange moon climbed the sky. Later the clearing would be as light as day. It should have been a beautiful evening, she thought numbly, a special night, celebrating her find.

At least she could share her discovery with Guy. She checked the fire, made sure the coffee pot was set firmly on the rock, and motioned for him to follow her again. "Guy, I've got something to show you." He looked at her curiously, but went along without question.

She had brought Roy Glen's big flashlight and between its light and the moon the woods were brightly lit. The grave wasn't far from camp. As she suspected, Roy Glen had probably been right when he said that their campsite was one the Indians favored long ago.

In the darkness of a tunnel of trees she made a couple of wrong turns, then found the dry creek bed. The flashlight beam caught the shovel, standing where she'd left it. Placing the light in Guy's hands in order to see what she was doing, she moved the shovel and then the branch away. She carefully brushed aside the dirt, then turned to Guy and smiled.

For a moment neither of them spoke. "Tessa." He exhaled the words as if he'd been holding his breath. "How? When?"

"This afternoon. A weasel helped me. She'd started a den, but I took it over when she left. I hope she found someplace else to sleep tonight."

"This is wonderful. How could you sit there and eat ice cream instead of telling me?"

"I—I wanted to show my daddy first."

When Guy put his arm around her, Tessa Mae realized she was shivering. But his embrace was warm and comforting.

"I'm sorry about Roy Glen, Tessa. Thank you for sharing with me."

They stood at the grave for a few minutes more before Guy spoke again. "Let's cover her back up until tomorrow."

"Why do you say *her*?" Tessa Mae asked. "How can you tell?"

"Wait here. I'll tell you later." He handed her back her flashlight, took his own, and headed to camp.

In a few minutes he returned with the tarp that Roy Glen usually spread on the ground under his blanket. They covered the grave with the cloth, anchoring it with a dead log and several big rocks to be sure an animal didn't find the skeleton and dig it out.

Back at the campfire, they opened a can of baked beans and a can of tuna. Guy had brought fresh cookies and a loaf of Wonderbread from town. They ate dinner in silence. Tessa Mae wadded up the soft bread and mopped the bean juice from her plate. She had been hungry. Now they sat sipping their coffee as the fire burned low and Tessa Mae asked again. "Why did you say cover *her* up, Guy?"

"I don't know. Just a hunch. Because you found her." He looked at Tessa Mae, his eyes making her feel warm way down inside—places where the coffee didn't reach.

"And why did you call me Tessa before?" She had to look away, so she poked at the fire and set her cup on the rock beside it.

Guy stood up and went over to the box he'd brought from town. He brought her a smaller box and then sat beside her. "Because it suits you. You're no longer that little girl I met a month ago. I thought maybe you hadn't looked at yourself since you got out here, so I got you this. Is it close to your birthday?"

Tessa Mae shook her head. Guy's sitting so close made her feel strange, like she wanted to laugh and cry at the same time. She wanted to jump up and run away. Instead, she opened the box and stared at the contents.

"November. My birthday is in November." Inside the box was a large, dark blue compact with a picture of a dogwood blossom on the front.

"Look in the mirror. There's a beautiful young woman there."

Tessa Mae didn't want to look at herself with Guy so near. Looking in a mirror was such a private thing. She felt self-conscious and silly. Taking a quick glance, she couldn't see that she looked any different. There was a smudge of dirt on her chin and her hair, escaping from the braid and curling around her forehead, looked frizzled.

"You shouldn't have brought me a present," she said,

closing the compact and running her fingers over the out-side. It felt as smooth as Mr. Inky's sleek skin. Had he forgotten her? she wondered suddenly. She had almost for-gotten him.

"It gave me pleasure, Tessa," he said, getting up to stand by the fire. "What are you going to do with the skeleton? And whatever else is in the grave?"

"Give it to Roy Glen, I guess. Maybe he'll let me keep something. Why?"

"It belongs to the museum. The archaeologists at the university should have a chance to study the skeleton."

"Did they send you down here to tell my daddy and me that what we're doing is wrong?" She returned the compact to its box.

"No, Tessa, of course not. I wanted to learn from your daddy. He really knows about the Indians who lived here. Some of my professors say he is *the* expert in this part of Arkansas."

Professors at the university thought her daddy was an expert on Arkansas Indians? Suddenly she wanted so badly for Roy Glen to see what she had found. Tears rolled down her cheeks and she couldn't stop them. She felt foolish and embarrassed sitting there in front of Guy, crying. Tessa Mae rubbed at her face with her arm.

Guy moved up beside her and put his arms around her. "Tessa, don't cry. Why are you crying? Because I brought you a present? I didn't know it would make you cry."

Although he was trying to make her feel better, it didn't seem to help. "I wanted my daddy to see what I'd found," she blurted out. "I wanted him to see it first. I wanted him to be proud that I'd found it." To her embarrassment, she started to cry even harder. It was as if everything that had happened to her lately, all the feeling she had pushed deep down inside to deal with later, had to get out right then, and she was powerless to stop the flood.

Guy sat with his arm around her until she began to regain control, then he said, "I know I'm not the same as your father, Tessa, but I'm glad you found the grave. I'm proud of you." He kissed the top of her head and held her even closer. "Roy Glen will be proud of you tomorrow when you show him."

"Yeah, I reckon—I mean, I know." Suddenly she felt uncomfortable with just the two of them sitting there alone. "We'd better get some sleep. We'll want to dig out the rest of the grave tomorrow." She pulled away, covering the glowing embers of the fire with ashes. Then she went to her blanket and lay down.

Instead of going off with his blanket, Guy took Roy Glen's spot. Tessa Mae wondered if he did that so she'd know where he was, so she wouldn't feel so alone. His gift of the ice cream, the compact, and now his thoughtfulness went a long way towards easing the tightness inside her. She lay quietly for a time until she could hear the steady breathing that signaled he was asleep.

But then, when she tried to sleep herself, she tossed and turned, trying to get comfortable. The army blanket scratched her bare arms and legs. A mosquito buzzed and whined at her ear. The cold, silver beams of the moonlight should have cooled off the night, but the air was heavy, oppressive. Perhaps she dozed, but it seemed to her that a mockingbird sang all night long. When it waked her at dawn, she felt soggy, and for the first time all summer she longed for her bed at home.

CHAPTER
TWENTY-ONE

"You up already?" Still groggy, Tessa Mae had expected to find Roy Glen at the campfire, but instead it was Guy who had the coffee ready. Its rich smell was the only thing that had persuaded her to get up.

"Too hot to sleep. Do the birds here always sing at night?" Guy yawned.

"That old mockingbird will sing anytime he feels like it." She took the cup Guy handed her, then found the canned milk and sugar so she could fix her coffee the way she liked it.

"Is there anyplace near here to swim?"

"There's a pond about a mile from here. Want to? I could use a bath," Tessa Mae answered.

"Me too. Let's go." Guy grabbed a towel and a bar of Ivory soap from the top of his backpack. Tessa Mae gulped her coffee and got ready to follow him, but she hesitated, wondering if she should check on Roy Glen. No, he'd just feel foolish if she were around when he woke up. So she scribbled a note telling him where they were and placed it near the coffee pot.

Tessa Mae worried about what to wear in the water all the way to the swimming pond. She didn't have a bathing suit, and she couldn't go in naked, that was for sure. She'd have no choice but to keep on her shirt and shorts.

The pond had never looked so inviting, shadowy and cool since the sun was still so low. "This is a great place!" shouted Guy. "Why haven't we been here before?" When he started undressing, Tessa Mae was relieved to see that he had on swimming trunks under his jeans.

Once in the water, Tessa Mae felt her clothes harnessing her like a plowhorse. Swimming this way wasn't loose and free as it was when she didn't have to worry about who was looking at her.

Guy laughed as he floated on his back, blowing water in a spurt like a whale.

"Ain't this fine?" she called to him from atop her big diving rock where she sat untangling her wet, unbraided hair with the comb she kept in the pocket of her shorts.

He climbed out beside her. "Sure is. We should come here every morning." His wet, brown body glistened in the early light. Looking at him did funny things to her stomach again, and she looked away, studying the hickory leaf ceiling and tugging at her hair.

"We wouldn't get any work done," she said, speaking carefully.

"Work, work, work. You're as bad as Roy Glen. Get up at dawn and go to work." He swooped her up and tossed her into the pond.

Sputtering and coughing, she came back to the surface,

angry as the old red squirrel who chattered in the tree overhead. "You . . . you . . . Yankee!" she screamed.

"Is that the worst thing you can think of to call me?" He laughed even more.

She reached over the smooth rock for his ankle, but he avoided her easily. Then she realized that her comb was gone.

Turning, she dived to find it, but when she held it in her hand and surfaced, Guy was gone. She pulled herself up and out, water dripping in a stream from her hair. Not bothering with a towel, she swung it behind her and shook like a wet dog.

By the time she had combed through her hair, Guy reappeared dry and dressed, his wet swimming trunks rolled neatly in his towel. She felt silly standing there so disheveled and wet.

"Roy Glen will think I kidnapped you. Don't know why he'd think I'd want such a pesky woman, though. One without sense enough to take a towel swimming." He unrolled his trunks and offered her the damp towel.

"I'll dry. I usually don't . . ." She realized what she was about to say and felt her face heat up.

"Wear any clothes?" He teased her with his eyes.

She looked away, then noticed that her wet shirt outlined her breasts worse than if she were naked. She pulled the wet cloth from her body and flapped it to dry as she walked ahead of him, leading the way on the narrow path.

Back at the campfire, Roy Glen sat, coffee in hand, head bent as if it hurt.

"Hey, Daddy, are you all right?"

"I reckon." He didn't look at them or say more.

Tessa Mae had decided to wait until after breakfast to tell her secret, but suddenly she was bursting with it.

Guy started the skillet of bacon, so she went down by

the river to change to dry clothing. A heron took off in slow motion, and a family of deer looked up from the riverbank, startled. Since she came down every morning to wash, however, the deer seemed to think she offered no threat. They entered the river to drink, ignoring her.

She changed quickly and hurried back, wanting to make sure that Guy didn't tell Roy Glen about her find. Guy handed her a plate of eggs, sunny side up, the way she liked them. The bacon was dry and crisp. But Roy Glen hadn't touched his breakfast.

She and Guy went to the river together, scooped up sand and scrubbed the egg and grease from their plates. Coming back up the hill, Guy brushed his hand across her hair, which she had left loose to dry. She shivered and hoped he didn't notice that his touching her made her feel so silly.

"It's pretty like that," he said. When she said nothing, he added, "Tell him, Tessa. He needs your news."

"I reckon he does." When they got to camp she crouched beside Roy Glen. He looked older than she'd ever seen him, older and more tired. "Daddy, I found something," she told him eagerly. "You have to come and see it."

"What is it, baby? What's the hurry?" His eyes were bloodshot, but there was a flicker of excitement there, too.

"You have to come with us to see it." She grabbed Roy Glen's hand and pulled at him as if she were a little girl. "Come on. Hurry."

Slowly he got up, put out his cigarette, and followed her. Guy, stopping to pick up a couple of shovels, hurried after them.

Tessa Mae uncovered the grave as if it were a wondrous work of art and she was showing it to the world for the first time.

"This is fine, baby. This is real fine." Roy Glen knelt and

brushed dirt from the skull. "It's old, I think, real old. I'm right proud of you, Tessa Mae. Right proud."

Tessa Mae smiled, waiting for him to say more. But he only said, "Let's get it dug out."

Tugging his old felt hat tighter, Roy Glen grabbed a shovel and started carefully to skin off the top layer of dirt. For a moment, Tessa Mae hesitated, then she followed his example, digging with Guy's shovel to excavate the skeleton.

The grave was only about two feet deep. Whether it had been dug shallow or the river had gradually eroded it, they might never know. By noon they were hot and sweaty, and the morning swim seemed days away. Tessa Mae had to stop and braid her hair, which was swirling around her face and sticking to her forehead and neck.

When they got close to the body, Guy joined in, the three of them digging with their hands. "Careful," instructed Roy Glen. "We don't want to break up the skeleton."

"There will probably be other things buried with her," Guy said.

"Is it a woman, Daddy?" Tessa Mae asked. "What do you think?"

"Probably. Look how small she was. And these are women's tools." Roy Glen took three bone hide scrapers from the dirt.

"Look," Tessa Mae whispered.

Curled into the arm of the skeleton was a tiny figure, its grave clothes rotted away so that only bones remained.

"It's a baby," Tessa Mae said in a hushed voice.

The woman had been buried in all her beaded finery, and shreds of suede leather and beads still clung to her bones. On one side of her body, close to the baby's head, was a broken dish, a piece of which had given Tessa Mae her clue to the grave. On the opposite side from the baby lay a perfect water jar, one of the prettiest that Tessa Mae had ever seen.

Carefully she lifted it out, brushing away the dirt that clung to the red and cream-colored sides. "What a wondrous thing," she said.

"It's beautiful, Tessa Mae," Roy Glen said. "A perfect piece. It's been years since I've found anything so fine. It's yours, of course. All this is yours. We'll need to build a crate to get it home."

Tessa Mae looked at the pot she held in her lap. A thin layer of red covered the jar in the same style as the broken dish. After the pottery maker had covered the cream-colored pot with red mud, she'd scratched through the red layer, drawing cardinals in a circle around the top. Deer danced around the fattest part of the jar in a graceful pattern.

Tessa Mae looked back into the grave. Ignoring the grinning skull, she imagined the woman lying there, clutching the infant that had probably killed her. Many Indian women died in childbirth. Had she made a beaded cradle like the beautiful one Roy Glen had sold? Had she fashioned the pottery jar to carry water from the river to bathe her child when it came? Tessa Mae felt tears course down her dusty cheeks, blending with the sweat.

She watched Guy, brushing dirt from the skeleton and wondered if he was thinking about his own mother who had also died in childbirth.

"I want to keep the pot, Roy Glen," Tessa Mae said. "But I'd . . . I'd like the bodies to go to the museum at the university." It was the best place for them to be. There other people could see that here was a mother who loved her child, just like any mother would. They could see that long ago, people were mostly the same as they are today.

Suddenly Tessa Mae had a vision of her own mother holding her baby, waiting in a lonely house for her husband to come home.

"You sure that's what you want to do, Tessa Mae? This is the best find I've seen lately, and these relics in here are worth a lot of money. Did you make up your own mind?"

Somehow taking money for the remains of the Indian woman and her child didn't seem right. Roy Glen thought Guy had helped her make the decision, but he hadn't. "I made up my own mind, Roy Glen," she told him. "I had all night to think about it. I'm sure."

"Think on it some more, but I've told you she's yours. Whatever you decide I'll have to go along with."

Through tear-filled eyes Tessa Mae saw Guy smiling at her. "I'll go get my towel. We can wrap the jar in it so we don't break it."

After Guy left, Roy Glen lit a cigarette and sat down on the creek bank to rest. "It's going to storm tonight," he predicted, wiping his head with a red bandanna. "Too hot. So we'd better cover the grave back up with the tarp and weigh it down with stones. I don't think we can get a box back here before night."

Guy came back with his towel which was still damp from swimming. The air was so full of moisture, nothing could dry. They wrapped the clay pot carefully, setting it under a nearby bush. Then the three of them spread the tarp over the grave, weighing it with stones.

Back at the camp they rolled up blankets, soaked the fires, and covered their supplies with an old checkered tablecloth that had a slick, waterproof coating. Guy hoisted his backpack and carried it to the truck. Tessa Mae carried the jar in her arms as carefully as she would a little child.

As they drove home, it occurred to Tessa Mae that she wouldn't mind showing Mama the water jar, but the rain was coming, and anyway she'd still be at work. They got home just as the storm hit. Tessa Mae stood at the door of her daddy's office and watched the rain pouring down, listened to the thunder crash. Roy Glen and Guy busied themselves with finding wood to build a crate.

The storm was over in an hour. Now the late afternoon was clear and fine. Tessa Mae sat on the back steps enjoying the cooled air as she watched water drip from the big oak, while a cardinal worked himself into a frenzy of singing. Other birds echoed its song, seeming to have enjoyed the rain as much as she had.

The moisture brought up the smell of roses and honeysuckle, and her mother's tiger lilies appeared refreshed, their bright orange trumpets nodding in the slight breeze. Suddenly, a voice broke through her reverie.

"Howdy, Tessa Mae I hoped you'd be here." Jec's face reflected the joy of the birds' singing. The anger he'd expressed when she saw him last seemed to be gone. Tessa Mae hardly knew him, though, he was so tall.

"Jec. You've been as scarce as hen's teeth. How's it going?"

"Everet got married and there's some extra space at our table. Mama figured as how you might be in the mood for some home cookin' if I could find you. I decided to try here first because you'd know it was going to storm bad."

"Boy, am I in the mood for Bertha's cooking." Tessa Mae remembered that she hadn't had any lunch. The idea of Bertha's corn bread made her mouth water and her stomach start to ache. "I got a new friend, Jec," she reminded him.

For a minute Jec hesitated, then said, "I figured that's why yer talkin' so fancy."

She smiled at that. Jec sure knew her well. "Can he come?"

Jec grinned back at her. "I reckon. Anythin' Miz Barbara Stanwyck wants is fine by me."

CHAPTER

TWENTY-TWO

She motioned for Jec to follow her to the shed where Guy and Roy Glen were building a crate.

"Daddy, Bertha has invited us to supper. It would be nice to get some good food. There's not much here to fix."

Roy Glen studied the frame of the wooden box for a minute. "I reckon that's a fine idea, Tessa Mae. I'm getting powerful hungry myself."

"Jec, this is my friend Guy." Tessa Mae introduced her two friends, one old, one new. Guy *had* become her friend in the last month. He was another person in her life whom she felt comfortable with.

Guy reached out to shake hands with Jec. Jec hesitated, then slowly put forth his hand.

"Pleased to meet you, Jec. I hear your mother is a great cook."

Jec studied Guy for a couple of seconds. "She sure is. And she caught a mess of catfish this mornin' before the storm. I had to clean all of them by myself."

Tessa Mae laughed, remembering the last time she and Jec had cleaned a mess of fish. "You should have had more brothers, Jec."

"I reckon you can say that again. What's that?" He nodded towards the box. "A coffin?"

"In a way," Guy said, then went back to helping Roy Glen finish the crate.

Tessa Mae told Jec about finding the grave.

"You could have helped us with the digging, Jec, but you never came down to visit at our camp."

"I had work to do, Tessa Mae. I've got a job now. I might not even go back to school next year." Jec pushed his hands in his pockets and stared at his bare feet.

"But Jec, you like school."

"Yeah, but maybe I like workin' too. Maybe I like havin' me some extra money."

Tessa Mae couldn't believe that Jec would really quit school, not after sixth grade. He could read as well as any eighth grader she knew. He'd liked the book about Mr. Darwin's explorations a lot, and sometimes Tessa Mae had lent him other books from her school library, because the few books the colored school had were old and worn-out.

Roy Glen and Guy stopped work and washed up. "We going to drive to the Browns'?" Tessa Mae asked.

"No let's walk now that it's cooled off some," Roy Glen suggested. Roy Glen and Guy stopped talking as they went single file down the path, watching the day shut down. Tessa Mae followed right behind Jec, but they didn't talk either. Something was gone for them now. When they reached the Browns', Jec disappeared.

Bertha hugged Tessa Mae and then put her to work in the hot kitchen where the good smells made Tessa Mae's stomach growl and rumble. Besides the wilted greens and hush puppies, Bertha had made applesauce cake with caramel icing and several cherry pies.

"I declare, Bertha. I feel like I've had nothing but beans to eat for a month." Tessa Mae watched the hot oil sizzle as Bertha dropped a glob of hush puppy batter off a big spoon. The batter puffed up and got little bumps on it as it swelled and fried.

"I told you to stop over. Where've you been, girl? I sent Jec to find you once." Bertha wiped her forehead with the tail of her big white apron.

"We were way down in the bottoms, south of you," Tessa Mae said. "It's a long way from here and the path winds around a lot. Unless Jec knew where we were, he could look forever." But Jec would have known where to look. He'd found them easily enough tonight. He seemed to be friendly one minute and angry the next.

"What were you all doing down there for a month?"

"Looking for Indian relics. I found a grave, Bertha. There was an Indian woman who died with her baby. There they lay all these years, waiting for me to find them."

"What fun is that, Tessa Mae? Diggin' up old graves. Girl like you could be workin' at somethin' in town. Yer mama shouldn't have let you go down there with yer daddy, sleepin' on the ground every night." Bertha poured hot bacon grease over the greens. "And that big old boy down there with you, too. Ain't natural or fittin' fer a girl as old as you. Look how you've turned into a woman since I saw you last. Tongues are goin' to start waggin'."

"I don't care, Bertha. I'm not doing anything wrong. I'm learning stuff that will be useful to me later."

Bertha shook her head. Tessa Mae knew that she would never understand, anymore than Mama would. Bertha scooped the last of the hush puppies from the pot with a slotted spoon and laid them on newspaper to drain.

"Rose Ann, get the men folks in here. Supper's ready."

Tessa Mae helped Bertha carry food to the table, and when Guy came in, she looked at him and smiled. He smiled back. She sat opposite him at the table, between Jec and Dee-Dee, and kept her eyes on the food, because every time she looked up, he was staring at her.

"You must be the best cook in Arkansas, Mrs. Brown," Guy said, reaching for another helping of catfish and taking two hush puppies at once onto his plate. "I've never had anything like this before."

"What do you eat in that place where you live?" Bertha asked. "Is there any good fishin'?"

"Yes, there's fish, and we have chowder. Clam chowder. And sometimes we have lobster."

"What's lobster?" asked Rose Ann and Dee-Dee together.

"Well, it's . . . it's red, or rather it's green until you cook it and then it's red."

Tessa Mae had seen pictures of lobsters in books. "It looks just like a huge crawdad, only it's colored different. It has big pinchers too."

"What a wonder," said Bertha. "And you eat it? Only raccoons eat crawdads."

"Yuk!" said Dee-Dee. "I wouldn't want to eat an old crawdad."

Guy grinned. "Lobster tastes really good. Maybe crawdads do, too. I know that people in Louisiana eat them." He held up what was left of his bread. "Why do they call these hush puppies?"

Rose Ann explained, "You throw one to the dogs when they're barkin' and you say—"

"Hush, puppy!" Dee-Dee finished, giggling.

Tessa Mae laughed too. Everybody was laughing, except Jec. He seemed even more grown-up since the day he accused her of not wanting to see him. Tessa Mae glanced at him anxiously, wishing he could like Guy and they could all be friends.

Roy Glen pushed away from the table. "I don't know if I can get up, much less speak."

"We've got pie and cake," Bertha said. "You cain't quit now."

"Gimme a minute, Bertha." Roy Glen got up. "I ain't sayin' no." He and Joses Brown went out onto the porch to smoke.

"I'll help clean up, Mrs. Brown," Guy offered. "It was a great meal."

"Plenty of women here, Guy. And everyone calls me Bertha. Miz Brown sounds like some lady I don't know. Maybe you and Jec could look after the little ones, though. With Florella gone, I could use another hand."

Tessa Mae, Bertha, and Rose Ann cleared the table. They pushed scraps into a pail for the pigs and chickens. Washing and drying the plates, they stacked them back onto the table for dessert.

"That's a right nice boy, Tessa Mae. You sweet on him?" Bertha asked.

"Maybe you'll go off and get married like Florella did," Rose Ann said.

"I sure won't do that." Tessa Mae felt her face grow hot. "He's just some boy who came from the university to help my daddy dig this summer. He said they know about Roy Glen up there."

"You don't say?" Bertha whisked dishes through the soapy water with lightning speed. "He ain't just some boy, though, Tessa Mae. He takes to you like a hog after persimmons. Maybe he came here to see your daddy, but now he's interested in other things."

"I can't see as how that's true." Tessa Mae kept her eyes on the glass she was wiping. "He'll go back to school soon, and I'll likely never see him again."

It was the first time she'd said it, but it was true. It was no use getting to like Guy a lot. He was being nice to her because she was the only girl around. When he got back to the university, there would be girls from the city who knew how to act around boys.

Everyone came back inside for dessert and coffee. Roy Glen had said he was full, but he managed both a piece of cherry pie and a slice of the applesauce cake. Guy and Jec did the same.

"I can see that no one likes my cookin'," Bertha said, laughing when plates were empty again, "so you'd jist better all git out of here." She refused any help with dishes. "Go on outside and enjoy this cool air while it lasts. I'll get me some good thinkin' done while I finish up."

The night air was soft and cool. Kerosene lanterns in the windows cast a warm glow onto the front yard. The Browns had electricity, but hadn't yet given up their lanterns.

Joses and Roy Glen leaned cane-bottom chairs against the porch wall and smoked. Guy and Jec sat on the steps watching Dee-Dee and Lilly Belle chase after lightning bugs, catch them, and put them in an old fruit jar. Baby Harry played in the dirt beside the steps.

"See my ring, Tessa Mae? Ain't it purty?" Dee-Dee held out her finger, glowing with a lightning bug's tail light.

Tessa Mae didn't want to tell her that she'd killed the bug by taking off its light. "Yes, Dee-Dee, but don't do it again. That little old bug needs his light to see to get home when you let him out of the jar."

They set the jar where Baby Harry could see it. He pumped his arms up and down and blathered about the bugs going on and off.

To Tessa Mae's surprise Jec suggested they play a game of hide and seek. But suddenly Tessa Mae felt too big to play. She wanted to keep sitting on the steps beside Guy.

"Oh, I'm too full to run, Jec. How can you move?"

"You can get hid and stay put. Come on, Tessa Mae." He pulled at her hand on one side and Dee-Dee started pulling on the other. "Come on, Tessa Mae," Dee-Dee and Lilly Belle said together.

"Can I play, too?" Guy asked.

"Sure," said Rose Ann. "But you're it. Last one playin' is it."

Tessa Mae couldn't believe that Guy wanted to play with them. She giggled, and ran to hide. Guy started counting. There was an unwritten rule about how far away they could go but Guy didn't know it, so she cheated a little. Down the path a ways, a wild hibiscus had spread out so wide that its branches hung over like a low umbrella. Tessa Mae burrowed under it, squealing quietly when she shook rain water from the limbs. The ground was damp, but she tucked her legs underneath her and sat, shivering, aware that the goose bumps on her arms and legs were caused by more than the cooled rain drops.

There was a funny feeling in her stomach that wasn't from eating too much supper. It was all she could do to relax and sit still. After a time she figured she was the only one still hidden and wondered if he'd given up. She waited for him to call, "Allie, allie, all's in free," and then she'd laugh because he hadn't found her.

But just as her legs felt too numb to stand, she heard

the soft crunch of footsteps on the path and then on the weeds near her hiding place.

The moon was still low in the sky, but her eyes had adjusted to the dark. She could see a dark shadow on the path. Should she sit still, she wondered, or try to get up and run past him?

In one motion he knelt beside the bush and caught hold of her arm. "You almost won," he said, pulling her to him. His mouth came down, warm and moist on hers.

Tessa Mae had never felt anything like the thrill that raced through her body. It was like diving to the bottom of the cool water in the swimming hole and hearing the calls of the first birds of spring all at once. It was like seeing an old red wolf playing with her babies, or holding a soft clutch of baby rabbits to her cheek.

Pulling Guy closer and feeling her body respond to his, she realized she was frightened. It was a wonder how natural and good it felt, but at the same time scary, something she should resist.

He pushed her gently from him, then scrambled up and ran away. She sat, frozen for a moment, then jumped to her feet and tried to follow. She stumbled along, twinges like pine needles jabbing her legs and feet as the blood raced back into them.

He was back in the Browns' yard by the chinaberry tree, when she got there.

"One, two, three for Tessa," he called out merrily.

"Where were you, Tessa Mae?" Jec asked. "You went too far." He sounded angry.

Had she gone too far? Had Guy gone too far, kissing her like that? Tessa Mae wouldn't give him another chance—or herself, for that matter—to find out. She was glad it was dark so he couldn't see her face.

Dee-Dee and Lilly Belle, as the first ones found, got to be "it" together. The others hid, making themselves easy to find. But when Tessa Mae got caught first, she said, "We'd better go on home, Roy Glen. It's getting late."

Bertha had joined the men on the porch, enjoying the night air, watching the hide-and-seek game. "It's early yet," she said. "You'd better enjoy this cool evening."

"You just want to go home so you won't have to be it," complained Jec.

"No such thing." Tessa Mae smiled at Jec's pouty face. If he was going to act so prickly, she'd ignore him. "Let's let the lightning bugs go home too, Dee." She grabbed the fruit jar and let Dee-Dee unscrew it. The bugs flashed their lights as they left. "They're saying good night. Good night, Rose Ann. Good night, Dee-Dee. Good night, Lilly Belle."

"Good night, Baby Harry," Lilly Belle said. "Good night, lightning bugs."

"See you, Jec," Tessa Mae called as they left the yard. She turned around, looked at Jec, and stood her ground, waiting.

Finally he reluctantly called back. "Not if I see you first."

Calling their thanks to Bertha, the three of them headed down the path towards the house where they'd decided to spend the night. Tessa Mae ran on ahead of Roy Glen and Guy, determined to get to her room before the others reached home.

She didn't want to risk being alone with Guy again tonight.

But even through her closed bedroom door, she heard him say,

"Good night, Tessa."

CHAPTER
TWENTY-THREE

Her bed felt so good she just lay there the next morning, stretching and being lazy. By the time she finally got up and reached the rain-washed light of the shed, she felt she'd dreamed the night before. Guy smiled and said good morning, but he was all business, sawing and hammering. He acted as if he'd never kissed her, or as if it meant nothing to him. Maybe it didn't. But it did to Tessa Mae. It was the first time a boy had kissed her. Was she being silly? Pushing it all aside to think about later, she plunged into the excitement of moving the grave.

By noon they had the finished crate loaded in the truck. They drove the long way through Lamar, in order to get as close as possible to their camp. Roy Glen and Guy unloaded the box and carried it while Tessa Mae walked ahead, pulling aside bushes and limbs, making room.

The hard, pounding rain had left only puddles in the stream bed and had done no damage to the grave because of the tarp covering it and the ceiling of leaves. Easing an old sheet beneath the two skeletons to keep from losing any bones, they lifted them into the crate. Then they gently wrapped the sheet over the remains of the woman and child. Tessa Mae collected the beads that had fallen from the rotted deer skin and were mixed with the dirt at the bottom of the grave. As she gently scooped them up in a sieve, she noted they were of many colors, suggesting that the design on the dress and moccasins had been carefully sewed, lovely in its pattern. The three bone scrapers and other tools were placed on top of the sheet and the beads put in a paper bag that Roy Glen had brought along.

It was late afternoon when they finally finished, so they decided to wait until morning for the drive to Fayetteville, where Guy had made an appointment with one of his professors. Tessa Mae looked at Guy as little as possible, feeling embarrassed about what had happened at the Browns'. Guy acted just as usual, which meant that the kiss must have been one of his playful whims.

The University of Arkansas looked like a cross between a park and a city. There were big buildings and green lawns and trees of every kind; the campus was landscaped like some of the big homes on the highway out of Lamar where rich people like J. H. Hamilton lived. Guy showed Roy Glen where to drive right up to the back of the science building. While Tessa Mae stood beside the truck and gawked at the campus view, Roy Glen and Guy unloaded the crate.

"Come on, Tessa Mae," Roy Glen said, when the double doors of the university building were braced open and they started into the building.

"Ain't—Isn't this fine, Roy Glen?" Tessa Mae stammered as they entered a building as big as Lamar High School. She followed them down the vast halls until Roy Glen and Guy stopped to leave the crate in one of the science laboratories.

"We're early," Guy said. "Professor Roberts is still in class. Want to get something to drink?"

"I'll stay here with the crate," Roy Glen said. He still wore his old felt hat. Tessa Mae wondered if he should take it off inside such a nice building.

"Come on, Tessa Mae," Guy urged, "I'll show you the rest of the building and the museum." And he started off down the hall.

"I especially want to show you the museum, since eventually that's where your find will go," Guy told Tessa Mae as they descended a long flight of stairs to a large entrance hall. Tessa Mae stared wordlessly at the glass cases that lined the entire room. They were full of displays of bones, pottery, models of Indian villages, dioramas of the woods and mountains environments with birds and animals that were native to Arkansas.

"You can look at the displays another time." Guy motioned for her to follow him as he entered a door marked "Employees Only."

In the rooms behind the displays new exhibits were being built. Tessa Mae stopped to watch a young man painting a backdrop for an Arkansas river scene. He looked up and smiled at her.

They moved on to see a boy about Guy's age stretching a black bearskin over a frame. "Hi, Guy," the boy said. "How's your summer going?"

"Not bad, Carl. This fellow going in the river exhibit?"

"If I ever get it finished."

"It's been a long time since I saw a black bear on my river," Tessa Mae said without thinking.

"Your river?" Carl tugged at the skin and Guy reached over to help him.

Guy laughed. "This is Tessa Ferris. She *owns* a whole stretch of woods near Lamar."

Tessa Mae felt her face getting hot. She was relieved when they left the museum and headed for the student union building.

"You could advise them on the river exhibit, I'll bet." Guy held the door for her as they entered the crowded snack bar.

"I could never do that, Guy," Tessa Mae said, staying right beside him. "Stop teasing me."

"I'm not teasing you. You probably know more about the woods and the river bottom country than anyone here. Do you realize you've identified every plant and tree and bush I've asked about this summer and told me more about the wildlife than I learned in a year's biology class? You could test out of all the botany courses and most of first-year biology."

"I couldn't even imagine going to school here, Guy," Tessa Mae said. "And working in that museum doesn't compare to finding a grave in the woods."

"Sure, being in the field and finding something exciting is the best part of being an archaeologist," Guy said over Cokes when they'd found a table. "But think of the days we hunted and found nothing."

"I always found something. We were outside, in the woods, seeing the birds and animals, hearing crickets and bird songs instead of cars and trash trucks like I do in the city."

"You were just enjoying being there, though. You weren't actually hunting for relics all that time," Guy argued. "Admit it, even finding the grave was an accident. You were watching that weasel."

Tessa Mae felt Guy had put her on the defensive. "What if I was?"

"An archaeologist has learned where to look, what to do with what he finds, what it means when he studies it. The people at the museum will put together the two skeletons you found. That means they have to have some knowledge of anatomy. They'll study the rest of the artifacts to decide what tribe the Indian woman belonged to, when she lived, how she died. You won't believe the information they'll come up with." Guy played with the paper his straw had come in, rolling it over his finger. "Could you do that? Could you put skeletons back together, reconstruct the scene? It really is necessary to study before you go out looking. You need to go to college, Tessa. It would be such a waste if you don't."

Tessa Mae thought Guy was getting awfully heated up about *her* life. She didn't like him calling her ignorant. "Roy Glen will teach me. Roy Glen knows more than anyone here. You said that yourself. He's an expert."

"How much good does that do other people, Tessa?" Guy leaned across the table to take her arm, but she pulled back. "Sure, he sells collectors a few arrowheads and rocks, and maybe even a pot or a cradleboard. But he's not contributing to history—the history of Arkansas and the people who once lived here. Why doesn't Roy Glen write down all he knows? He could write some books that would help other people, not just students, but everyone in Arkansas who would like to know about the past. What if Roy Glen died tomorrow? All he knows would die with him. Then what good did it do for him to know it?"

"He would have enjoyed knowing it for himself."

"There's nothing wrong with that, Tessa. But he has a responsibility to share what he knows." Guy was speaking so loudly that students around them turned and stared.

Tessa Mae became aware of how she looked in her shorts and ugly, worn-out shoes. She'd seen a couple of girls in shorts, but most wore dresses. She wanted to curl up and become invisible, but instead Guy was actually calling attention to her. They finished their Cokes in silence, a trace of animosity lingering between them. One thing was sure. She wasn't going to let him talk her into doing anything she didn't want to.

Back at the science lab, they found Roy Glen talking to Professor Norman Roberts. Guy introduced her as Tessa, leaving out the "Mae."

"I confess I couldn't wait, Miss Ferris. I dismissed my class early and came to look at your find."

They gathered around the opened crate, looking at the skeletons and the relics from the grave, except for the water jar which Tessa Mae had left in her father's office.

"This is the most complete grave anyone's found for a long time," the professor said, his eyes shining. "I'd like to congratulate you, Miss Ferris, on your discovery."

"A weasel helped me," Tessa Mae responded.

Professor Roberts laughed. "It won't be the first time an animal has helped in a discovery. Not long ago a cave was discovered in northern Arkansas because a cow fell into it, or practically into it. Fortunately for the cow, the hole wasn't that big. And we're especially pleased that you're willing to donate your find to our museum here at the university, Miss Ferris."

Tessa Mae nodded in acknowledgment of his thanks. "I wanted other people to see it," she said softly. "To see the mother and baby."

"You appear to have some of your father's luck and skill at finding relics, Miss Ferris. Have you thought about where you're going to college? A student with your background would certainly be welcome here."

"I don't expect to go to college," she said. She glanced at Roy Glen, but he was studying the skeleton and didn't look up.

"Tessa—may I call you that?" The professor was speaking very seriously. "Let me say again how much this contribution means to the museum. Your discovery will attract students and archaeologists from all over the state. Your age—the fact that you yourself are a student—will be a strong argument for more scholarship money, too. Sometimes I have to convince the university administration of the need to recruit young people like you."

Tessa Mae looked at her feet, embarrassed, as the professor continued to speak.

"I can't stand the idea of your not going to college, Tessa. Is it . . . Is it . . ." He looked from her to Roy Glen. "Is it a matter of finances? What if I could get you a scholarship covering full tuition, and room and board, on the basis of this discovery?"

"I reckon I can pay for Tessa Mae's schoolin' if she wants to go to college," Roy Glen said. Tessa Mae could hear the pride in his voice.

"Then I could apply for a scholarship that pays tuition and books, Mr. Ferris. It'd be easier to get." The professor spoke animatedly as if she were already enrolled. "You can pay for room and board or Tessa Mae can work for it."

"Do we have to decide today?" she asked Professor Roberts.

"Of course not. Don't you have some high school left?"

"Four years." The professor must think she was older

than fourteen. Four years seemed to Tessa Mae like a lifetime. It was hard to even imagine it.

"I'm going to put your name on a plaque by this display, Tessa. It will say that you found this gravesite and donated its contents to the museum. Your father gave me the details of the site, and what tribe he thinks it is from, but we'll do a lot of studying before we say for sure. You can come and visit your discovery whenever you like."

Tessa Mae was pleased both by his invitation and by having her name on the plaque. Maybe she'd tell her mother to have Dixie Lee drive her over to see it. It was proof that she hadn't been wasting the summer. Even Roy Glen didn't have a display in the museum with his name on it.

Roy Glen walked back to the truck quickly, as if he were anxious to leave.

"I'll buy lunch at the cafeteria," Guy suggested. "How about it, Roy Glen? Let's celebrate."

"I've got some business in town," Roy Glen said. "I'll come back for you later."

Tessa Mae had a feeling that Roy Glen was lying. "We could go on home," she offered.

"No, you go with Guy, Tessa Mae, and celebrate like he says," Roy Glen lit up a cigarette and climbed in the truck, the matter settled.

Tessa Mae watched him drive away, wanting to shout, "I'll go with you." She felt awkward and out of place here despite Guy's company.

"See there," Guy said, not picking up on Tessa Mae's uneasiness. "The university would even offer you a scholarship."

They strolled across the campus where a few students lingered in the shade of the big trees. Tessa Mae knew it would be horrible to have to sit in classes all summer.

"I never said I'd take it." Tessa Mae wiped her hands on her shorts, feeling sticky and hot.

They went back to the student union grill where Tessa Mae ordered a cheeseburger and some french fries.

"Hey there, Guy." The pretty girl who handed the food to Tessa Mae smiled. He smiled back. "Shirley, hi. How's your summer going?"

Tessa Mae couldn't help but compare herself to the girl. She had on a red cotton circle skirt and a frilly white blouse covered by an apron, but Tessa Mae could tell that they were store-bought, probably from a nice store. Her hair was black, straight, and glossy. Tessa Mae had unbraided hers, but now wished she hadn't. She had tried to tame it with a red ribbon, but it kept slipping loose and flying in all directions. She'd been foolish to think that Guy could like her when there were pretty girls everywhere on campus.

"All the people who work here are earning money toward their schooling, Tessa. You could work here for room and board." After seeing that Tessa Mae had catsup, Guy bit into his hamburger.

Tessa Mae ate, watching the summer school students come and go. They all seemed happy, laughing and chattering and calling to each other as if everyone knew everyone else. There were as many people in the cafeteria as lived in the whole town of Lamar, and this was just the summer session.

Two people, Miss Criswell and Guy, had already encouraged her to go on past high school. Now Professor Roberts has said he could hardly stand to think of her *not* going to college. But the thought of high school scared her enough. College would be terrifying. It would be easier to live with Roy Glen and spend most of her time in the woods. Right now that was all she wanted to do.

Guy did the talking at lunch. When students stopped by their table to visit, he always introduced her, but no matter how friendly they were, Tessa Mae felt self-conscious and out of place.

They met Roy Glen outside the science building. Everyone seemed lost in his own thoughts as they drove back to Lamar and stopped at the post office. There was a square white envelope for Tessa Mae among Roy Glen's mail, an invitation to Miss Criswell's wedding in Clarksville. It was Tessa Mae's first wedding invitation. If it was like the weddings in movies, she definitely wanted to go.

It would be fun to see Miss Criswell in a pretty white dress and veil, with everyone throwing rice at her and Judge Noble. It struck Tessa Mae as funny that she'd never seen any divorces in the movies—even movies in which bad things happened. Divorces must be something people wouldn't go to the movies to watch. Guy was saying something to her.

"What?" Tessa Mae said.

"I said, I'd be pleased to escort you. To the wedding, I mean."

"That would be nice," she said to Guy. "Yes, I'd like that."

She'd made up her mind about something else. "You and Guy get the groceries, Roy Glen," she said. "I'm going by to see Mama like I promised." It was about four-thirty, so Mama would probably just be getting home from work.

Sure enough, she was sitting at the kitchen table, drinking a Coke, still in her work clothes. She looked tired.

"Hi there, Mama. We've been to Fayetteville. You'll never guess why."

"I reckon I couldn't, Tessa Mae. You doing all right?" Her mother didn't seem particularly interested in what Tessa Mae had to tell her.

"I'm fine, Mama. I found a grave." Tessa Mae told her

mother all the details of the Indian woman and her baby and the pottery and the beads.

"That's nice." Her mama hardly looked at Tessa Mae the whole time she told her story. Nice? Tessa Mae stared at her. Was that all her mother could say about the most exciting thing that had ever happened to her?

Mama showed the same lack of interest in Miss Criswell's wedding. Tessa Mae got up and went to her room to get the blue dress. There was nothing else to say. She watched her mother circle the soda bottle with hands that were wrinkled from being in water all day. There were dark circles under her eyes.

"Are you feeling okay, Mama?" Tessa Mae asked. "Are you happy in town?"

"I reckon. I can count on things."

"Well, I'd better be going." Tessa Mae stood up, giving Mama a minute to say more. When she didn't, Tessa Mae said, "Roy Glen and Guy are buying groceries. They'll be waiting for me."

"You gettin' enough to eat?" Mama asked, still not looking at her.

"Sure. Roy Glen and Guy can both cook, but I do most of it. We take turns cleaning up. Well . . . I'll see you the next time we come to town."

"All right, Tessa Mae." Her mother didn't even get up from the table, so Tessa Mae let herself out and ran down to Miller's where she'd promised to meet Roy Glen and Guy. The visit had left her with an empty feeling, but she put it aside for now.

"We ran into Maudie," Roy Glen told her. "How about eatin' supper there?"

"Great. I haven't seen enough of them lately."

It pleased Tessa Mae that Guy fit in at Elbert and Maudie's just like he had at the Browns'. Maudie made him eat two pieces of chocolate pie and then he dried dishes while Elbert and Roy Glen visited together on the front porch.

"That's a nice young feller," whispered Aunt Maudie when Guy went outside to join Elbert and Roy Glen.

"Roy Glen likes him," Tessa Mae said as she helped put away dishes.

"You don't?" Aunt Maudie teased. "Thought it was him turned you into a lady."

"I like him some. He finds lots of good stuff when we're digging."

Aunt Maudie shook her head as if to say things were sure different from when she was a girl.

"If I was around here much, I'd get too fat for a boy friend." Tessa Mae and Maudie laughed at the notion of a fat Tessa Mae.

"What's so funny?" Guy asked when he and Roy Glen came back in the kitchen.

"Nothing much. Carrying all those groceries in the dark's gonna be fun," Tessa Mae said, reminding them of the time.

"I'd carry them two miles for a dinner like that." Guy thanked Maudie and Elbert and they all climbed back into the truck.

Tessa Mae worried about her mother on the silent trip back to camp. Maybe Mama was just tired because she'd just got home from work, but she didn't seem happy. She'd said she was, but Tessa Mae figured she'd hate to admit it if she wasn't. There didn't seem to be much Tessa Mae could do.

After helping unload the groceries, Tessa Mae realized how tired she was. She spread out her blanket and was asleep almost immediately. By the next morning she was impatient to get back to exploring.

They spent the last weeks in July digging near where Tessa Mae had found the grave, then moved up on Mr. Klauber's farm. Mr. Klauber thought he'd found another grave, but after examining it, Roy Glen said animals had probably dug it up before. There were a few scattered bones and some broken pottery bits, but not enough to piece together and glue.

Tessa Mae's mind wandered the whole time they poked around Klauber's field. The wedding, the divorce, her going off to college some day to become a famous archaeologist—all these things swirled round inside her head. Once, she even dared to dream that she and Guy would have a wedding someday. They'd be a famous team, discovering incredible relics in Arkansas and then going to foreign lands to dig, too.

It was hard to keep the dream about Guy going full speed, though. Ever since that kiss that both pleased and scared her, he'd treated her like his kid sister again. Sometimes they could talk seriously around the campfire at night after Roy Glen had gone to bed, but he never acted like he wanted to kiss her again. She looked at her compact often. It was a thoughtful gift, but giving it to her must have meant nothing else to him except kindness.

One day they were wandering together along the winding creek that ran into the river below their camp. There wasn't much water left in it on account of its being late July, so it was perfect for wading and cooling off her feet.

"Look, Guy, it's a wishing rock." Tessa Mae picked up the flat stone, water-smoothed, which had a perfect circle eroded in its center. "You want to wish on it?"

"You found it, Tessa. You wish. Ask for something you really want."

The way he kept calling her Tessa was beautiful whether

he said it as if she were his little sister or not. He made her name sing softly like dry leaves whispering in a fall breeze.

"I wish my mama and my daddy would go back together," Tessa Mae said, without throwing the rock. "I wish I didn't have to choose between them."

"You're not really choosing between the two of them as persons," Guy said. "You're choosing who you'll live with for the next four years. You can still spend time with both of them. You should be glad you have a choice, a say in your own life. Most people don't get much choice about a lot of things that happen to them."

"Maybe it would be easier if the judge chose for me."

"Sure, it would be easier, but you don't want to let him do that, do you?"

She shook her head, agreeing, then asked, "What do you think I should do?"

"It's not my decision."

"You must have an opinion. I know you do."

"I think you should keep going to school, no matter who you live with." Guy picked up a flat stone and skipped it down the creek. "I think you shouldn't keep running wild down here in the river bottoms."

"Why not?" she said rebelliously. "You just now said I had a choice. Why can't I choose living down here forever?"

She rubbed the smooth wishing stone, poking her little finger through the center hole. Deciding to keep it, she dropped it into her pocket and sat down, leaning on a tree near the creek. She put her head down on her knees, wanting to cry really hard or hit at something. The judge's words about someone being too mixed up or involved to make the right decision came back to her. She understood what he meant now.

Guy sat beside her and put his hand on her shoulder. "I wish I could help you, Tessa. But I can't. No one can."

She looked at his blue eyes and reached up and smoothed the frown from his forehead. "I know. Do you like me, Guy?"

He took away his hand and studied his bare feet. "Yes, Tessa, I do like you. I like you a lot. You're different."

"You like me because I'm different? What a wonder. I figured you'd like one of those town girls better, like the one who smiled at you. One of those pretty girls from the university who talks right all the time and acts citified, not like a running-wild-in-the-woods girl."

He smiled. "Pretty doesn't have anything to do with liking someone, Tessa. But you are pretty, even more so because you don't realize it. There's a beauty in you that's like these woods—a beauty no town girl can match and no amount of schooling or city life can take away."

He pulled her to him and kissed her. Not a kiss like before, but one that was gentle and sweet—a kiss that was the beginning of his saying good-bye.

CHAPTER
TWENTY-FOUR

Guy took Tessa Mae to Miss Criswell's wedding, just as he'd promised. It was as good as any Tessa Mae had seen in the movies. She cried almost all the way through the ceremony, and Guy teased her about being so sentimental. She couldn't help it. Miss Criswell had on the prettiest dress Tessa Mae had ever seen. It was made of lace worn over a satin slip, and the lace sleeves came to points at the wrist. Her veil puffed around her face and trailed out clean down her back. But best of all Miss Criswell looked as if she was about to burst with happiness, and Tessa Mae liked to think she'd find that happiness for her own life someday.

"How are you doing this summer, Tessa Mae?" Judge Noble asked her at the reception, which was held in the basement of the church. "Are you living in the river bottoms with your father as you wanted?"

"Yes, sir, I am, and this here—this is Guy Eliot from the university. He's helping us dig Indian relics. The . . . the present I brought you . . . I found it myself in a grave this summer."

"Sharon." Judge Noble motioned for Miss Criswell—now Mrs. Noble, Tessa Mae reminded herself—to come over to the table which was piled high with gifts.

Mrs. Noble smiled at her new husband, then at Tessa Mae and Guy. "I'm so glad you could come, Tessa Mae."

"Tessa Mae brought us a present that she found herself, Sharon." Judge Noble pointed to the present, wrapped in plain brown paper. "Let's open it now."

"Of course." Mrs. Noble tore at the paper, then opened the pasteboard box carefully. "Oh," she whispered. "Oh, Tessa Mae, this is so special. Are . . . are you sure you want us to have it?" She pulled out the water jar and turned it round and round, running her fingers over the sides.

"I'm sure." Tessa Mae had never felt so proud. Mrs. Noble knew it was special. Tessa Mae could tell by her face, the tears in her eyes.

Setting the water jar back on the table carefully, Sharon Noble gathered Tessa Mae in her arms, and hugged and kissed her. "I'll treasure it forever, Tessa Mae."

The couple didn't open any more presents but left as soon as Mrs. Noble had changed into her traveling clothes, a blue suit that matched her eyes. Tessa Mae threw her handful of rice and laughed as the newlyweds squealed and ducked and ran for Judge Noble's car.

She carried the warmth in her heart to the restaurant where Guy took her for dinner.

"You were the prettiest girl at the wedding, Tessa," Guy said as they waited for their food.

Tessa Mae felt almost pretty in her blue dress, sitting there with Guy, pretending this was a real date. Her daddy had given her money for new sandals. She'd bought white ones without worrying that the thin straps wouldn't last very long. She didn't feel out of place in the elegant restaurant.

She wondered, though, if new clothes were going to help her much this fall—help her go to high school and feel comfortable there. She felt as if her very skin was too tight, as if she was growing on the inside even faster than she was outside. Somehow she no longer was that little girl who wanted to do nothing except swim with Jec and sit in a grape arbor and read—a little girl who thought she could go off and live in the woods forever.

As if he could read her mind, Guy said, "Don't change too much, Tessa."

"I'm going to have to change some, aren't I?"

"I guess so, but I'll miss the girl I've spent the summer with, the Indian princess I found in the woods in June."

Tessa Mae ate quietly, knowing the time was coming for her parents or a judge to decide what to do about her. She didn't believe she'd really have a say.

"It'll be all right, Tessa," Guy said, after their silent drive home. "Whatever happens, I know you'll be all right." He leaned over and brushed his lips against her cheek.

She took her sleeping blanket down to the river that night, needing to be alone. She had cried easily and a lot all summer, but now the tears had stopped. The trouble was, it seemed as if they were all gathered up in a tight ball in her throat.

The next day, after breakfast, Guy told her he was leaving at the end of the week to visit his father and get ready for the fall term at the university.

"I know. Will you come back to visit?" she asked. "We could dig on the weekends."

"I probably will, Tessa. Even though I went all summer

finding only the two spear points. That is, if I don't count the beautiful girl I found roaming the river bottoms." He smiled, teasing her.

"Running wild, you mean." Tessa Mae reminded him. "I hope she counts for something."

"Not only does she count for a lot, she's going to be a great archaeologist someday."

"I reckon." Tessa Mae said on purpose, with a grin. But Guy's eyes had turned serious.

"Just to remind you not to change too much I got you a present." He held out a long box wrapped in white tissue with a green bow.

"What is it? I didn't get you anything."

"That's okay. Open it."

She tore off the paper and ribbon to find a store-bought fishing pole and reel. She put the pieces of the pole together and flexed it in her hand. "Thanks," she said in a half whisper, then, mocking her old way of speech, "I'll catch me some big catfish for sure now. More than I did this summer with my old cane pole."

"And maybe Bertha will cook them up along with some of her famous hush puppies," Guy said.

"Guy . . . Guy . . . I . . . Here." Tessa Mae dug deep in her shorts pocket. "You take my wishing stone. Wish for everything you've ever wanted. Wish your way back here someday."

Her hand brushed his and she jerked away, taking the pole and running. She didn't want him to leave, ever. She ran all the way to her favorite fishing hole, then stumbled. Only then did she let go of the tears. She sunk down on the ground and clasped her knees to her chest.

Right now it felt like she'd never see Guy again. But no, she couldn't think that, she couldn't. Maybe some day she'd be sitting here on the riverbank, fishing. She'd hear this noise, like wind whispering in the willows. It would be him. "Tessa," he'd say. "Howdy, Tessa. How's fishing? I came back to see if you caught that big one you were after."

She blinked her eyes free of tears and brushed the back of her hand over her cheeks. It felt comforting to be near the fishing hole where she and Bertha and Jec had caught so many fish. Finally she slept through the heat of the heavy August afternoon. When she woke, her mouth was dry and tasted bitter and her clothes were soaked with sweat.

Leaving her pole on the bank, she pulled off her clothes and slipped into the river. The warm water refreshed her and she floated on her back, barely kicking. A bit cooler, she put her shorts back on, but dipped her blouse in the water, then wrung it out. While it hung on a bush to dry, she twisted another worm on the shiny new hook and tossed it back into the water. By the time she had pulled in enough fish for their dinner, she'd done a lot more thinking—not about Guy—but about herself. She knew what choice she had to make. Maybe she'd known it all summer.

She was glad that Guy was gone when she got back to camp. Saying good-bye over and over all week would have been hard. But finding a note pleased her.

> *Dear Tessa,*
> *It seemed right for me to go ahead and leave today. I have the wishing rock in my pocket. I'll wish myself back. I promise.*
>
> > *Love,*
> > *Guy*

Tessa Mae folded the note and tucked it in her pocket. Then she cut up the fish, having cleaned them at the river, rolled the chunks in cornmeal, and put them in the skillet to fry. Peeling potatoes, she added them to the skillet. Before long Roy Glen strolled into camp.

"Guy's left," Tessa Mae said without looking at her daddy.

"I figured it'd be soon. He said he had to go home before school started. Dinner smells good, Tessa Mae. I'm powerful hungry." Roy Glen sat down and lit a cigarette.

After supper, Tessa Mae broke the silence between them. "Daddy, Guy said you should write a book about the Indians that lived here, so other people could learn what you know." She watched him light another of the Camels.

"I couldn't write no book, honey. I wouldn't even know where to start. I never had all that schoolin' you're gonna get."

"Do you wish you had gone on and finished school, Daddy? Do you wish you could write a book?"

"Ain't no use thinkin' and wishin' about what could have been."

"Are you happy, Daddy? Are you happy doing what you're doing? Hunting around down here for Indian relics, trading and selling what you find?"

Roy Glen studied the fire and took a long drag on his cigarette, blowing smoke at the mosquitoes that were pestering them. "I reckon so. I reckon it's enough."

Just three months ago Tessa Mae had thought that what Roy Glen was doing would be enough for her. She'd thought his kind of life was the finest thing she could imagine. Now she knew it wouldn't be right for her.

It was too hot to sleep. The same mockingbird who'd lived near them all summer kept talking about how hot it was. Mosquitoes buzzed and whined around her ears. She kept kicking off her blanket, knowing that the bugs would have her bare legs looking like she had the measles.

Finally, just as the sky started to turn to another blue-hot day, she made up her mind. Digging out her notebook, she scribbled a note to Roy Glen.

> *Dear Daddy,*
> *I've decided to go live with Mama in town*
> *after all. That doesn't mean I won't see you a*
> *lot too. I'll come down here every weekend and*
> *when the weather gets bad I'll come to the*
> *house and help you with your orders. I'm plan-*
> *ning to keep going to school. Maybe someday*
> *I'll even help you write a book.*
> *Cause I love you.*
>
> *Tessa Mae*

She bundled up her gear into the army blanket and slung it over her shoulder. Then as quietly as an old red wolf, she slipped away onto the path towards the house and then walked on into town.

Her mother was getting ready for work when Tessa Mae opened the door and came in without knocking. "Tessa Mae, what are you doin' here so early in the mornin'? Is anythin' wrong?" She motioned for Tessa Mae to sit down and poured her a cup of coffee. It didn't taste as good as the coffee they made on the campfire, but it was hot and sweet.

"I'm home, Mama," Tessa Mae said. "I'm home for good because I'm going back to school this fall. I'm going to need some new clothes. I'm sorry. I can probably get some money babysitting soon and pay you back, and Roy Glen owes me some money, too."

"That's okay, baby. I'll buy you some new clothes. Oh, I'm so glad, Tessa Mae. I've missed you so much." Her mother lit up like the sun coming up on a new day. Some of the sunshine from her mama's smile warmed Tessa Mae, too.

Tessa Mae stepped over, put her arms around her mother, and said, "I want you to call me Tessa, Mama. Not Tessa Mae. 'Cause that's who I am now. Tessa."

Her mother didn't call her anything right then because she was crying. Tessa Mae sat back down at the table. She tried to sip coffee past the lump in her throat. "Hadn't you better get ready for work, Mama? I don't want to make you late."

Her mother nodded and dabbed at her eyes. "Maybe I can take part of today off, Tessa Mae . . . Tessa," she said, trying out the new name. "We got lots of shopping and planning to do. I can fix—"

"I'll be here when you get home, Mama. I've some things to do." Tessa Mae watched her mother go into the bathroom to wash her face. Then she got out her new fishing pole and calling, "See you later," she took off back down towards the woods.

She might not be welcome as far as Jec was concerned, but going to his house was what she felt like doing. She'd bet Jec was still sleeping. Not even a job could change him from sleeping as late as he could.

She slipped up to his window just like old times, settling back into the familiar speech. "Jec, hey, Jec. Wake up in there, you hear?"

When Jec came to the window, rubbing the sleep from his eyes, he stared at her as if he was still dreaming. "Tessa Mae?"

"Come on out here, Jec. I got me somethin' to show you."

In a couple of minutes, Jec appeared, pulling up the straps on his overalls. "I never expected to see you here this mornin', Tessa Mae," he said. "What you got there? Whoooeee, what a fishing pole. Can I hold it?" He was acting as if they'd never been apart.

"Sure." She handed him the pole. He took a good hold on it, flicked it a few times to get the feel of it, then ran his hand over the smooth rod.

"Your mama home?" Tessa Mae asked, leaning against the porch railing.

"Nah, she's already gone, maybe to the peach shed. But she's been workin' a lot lately. Lots of white people have dirty houses for her to clean." Jec seemed to step away from Tessa Mae when he said that, and his voice sounded angry. He handed back the pole. Maybe he remembered that Tessa Mae was white folks, too.

Tessa Mae took it reluctantly. "I reckon you can't go fishin' then."

Jec sat on the porch steps. His knees stuck up in the air like a grasshopper's. There were holes in the knees of his overalls. "I reckon not. Besides, I have to go to work pretty soon myself." He didn't look at Tessa Mae, and she had run out of anything to say.

"Maybe if I catch me a whole bunch of catfish, I'll come back and leave some here for your supper. I'm livin' with Mama now, and we can't eat but two."

"You ain't gonna live in the woods with your daddy?"

"No, I guess I'll go on to school when it starts, so I'll have to stay in town." There was another uncomfortable silence. "You goin' to school this fall, Jec?" Tessa Mae asked.

"I reckon so. My mama is set on it."

Knowing Bertha, and remembering her determination to have one of her children finish high school and maybe even go to college, Tessa Mae figured Bertha would keep being set on it. But Jec would have to make that decision for himself like she had when the time came.

"Well, I'll see you." Tessa Mae stood up to leave but Jec kept sitting on the steps.

Just as she was almost out of the yard, he called to her. "Not if I see you first, Tessa Mae." She looked back and he was grinning.

Her heart lifted a little. Maybe she and Jec couldn't be best friends anymore, but she hoped they could still see each other sometimes.

And she'd let him call her by her old name. She'd tell the teachers at school and any new friends she might make to call her Tessa, but Jec and Roy Glen could keep on calling her Tessa Mae.

After all, she didn't want to change so much she'd forget who she'd been for all these fourteen years.